Motocross Mike

By

Charles Loomis

authorHOUSE

1663 LIBERTY DRIVE, SUITE 200
BLOOMINGTON, INDIANA 47403
(800) 839-8640
www.authorhouse.com

This book is a work of fiction. Places, events, and situations in this story are purely fictional and any resemblance to actual persons, living or dead, is coincidental.

© 2004 Charles Loomis.
All Rights Reserved.

No part of this book may be reproduced, stored in a retrieval system, or transmitted by any means without the written permission of the author.

First published by AuthorHouse 05/20/04

ISBN: 1-4184-5064-2 (sc)

Printed in the United States of America
Bloomington, Indiana

This book is printed on acid-free paper.

Dedicated to the memory of

Gregory Putman

December 2, 1963 – April 12, 1978

CHAPTER ONE

The sound of engines reached a whining peak as each rider strained forward with his eye on the starting gate. Forty motocross bikes lined up side by side, their riders twisting throttles, on and off to higher and higher rpm's until it seemed that every engine on the start line would blow up in a thick cloud of blue smoke. The gate dropped.

Forty clutches were popped by forty fast left hands. Forty rear wheels churned the dirt and grass of the start line into plumes behind powerful motocross bikes.

Mike was a fraction of a second quicker. He let out his clutch earlier than everyone else on the line. His weight was positioned perfectly for just the right amount of traction and it put him in the lead. He had the "hole-shot" and would be the first one to the track entrance, a tricky, ninety-degree turn onto a thirty foot wide course.

Charles Loomis

Mike was pleased with himself. "That start should to impress the factory boys," he thought, remembering the Honda factory representatives who were there to watch him race. His life's ambition was to get sponsorship and ride the national circuit the following season. This was his big chance to impress the factory "reps".

He led the pack almost to the first turn. Then, as he began to shift his weight forward for the turn onto the track, his front wheel hit a rock hidden in the grass. The front forks bottomed out and he slid violently up the gas tank to the handlebars. His mid-section hit the bars and he felt the rear wheel rise slowly into the air. He was going to "endo" and he knew it.. In horrifying slow motion, he was down.

He felt his sponsorship slipping away because of his stupidity. He couldn't believe this was happening. He hung on to the handlebars with all his strength to control his fall. He needed all the leverage he could get to twist out from under the bike. The bike began the first of three end-to-end tumbles. His feet were in the air, a handstand on the handlebars of a motorcycle gone wild.

His back hit the ground with a thud and Mike's breath whooshed out of his chest. For a moment stars whirled in his vision and he thought he would black out.

The bike was coming down on him. In a split second he'd pushed it away and twisted to one side. The back end crashed to

Motocross Mike

the ground just inches from his left foot, tearing loose the fender and bending the rear frame as if it was a soda straw. The bike flipped again, jerking Mike up, his legs flailing to the side. The force was more than he could cope with. He lost his grip on the bars and again hit the ground. Luckily, he landed to the side of the bike, rolled and lay still, frightened that he might be badly hurt.

His accident hadn't slowed anybody down. The race was still on. Bill Maslak, had told him a long time ago that "nothing stops the start in motocross unless a lot of guys jump the gate." Bill knew what he was talking about. He was an ex racer himself and the owner of the cycle shop where Mike worked.

"Press," he'd told Mike. "Keep pressing no matter what happens around you."

And Mike always did. It was one of the reasons he was so often a winner and was now in the "Expert" class. He had seen riders down on that first turn just like he was now. Stalled, handlebars and footpegs locked together, straining and pulling at one another while other riders tried to avoid them. Mike would ride around them too, pushing and pressing other riders out of his way. Riders and motorcycles might be hurtling through the air, but he always kept his eye on the line.

Now on the ground, he forced himself to focus on the horde of other riders coming toward him. They'd been told the same thing that Bill had told him - "press", and Mike knew he had to defend

Charles Loomis

himself. No rider would intentionally run over another, but in the smoke, dust and confusion of the start, anybody could make a mistake. He'd been in the lead and now a howling mass of men and dirt bikes was bearing down on him at terrifying speed. Too late to get to the side of the track, Mike tried to shield himself with the bike now lying twisted and broken on the ground.

Having seen Mike go down, the riders in the middle of the pack were pushing and elbowing to the right and left in order to get by him. The lead riders passed him easily. One, two, three to the left, two to the right.

Mike watched helplessly as the main pack roared toward him. These riders were the ones to worry about. The dust from his crash and the race made him practically invisible.

Ready to jump in either direction, Mike watched and listened as the screaming bikes approached with increasing speed. The ones in the middle could do one of three things - push to either the right or left and hope the bikes to the side would yield, they could stop, or they could miss seeing Mike altogether and slam into him.

It had all happened in an instant, but Mike felt like it would never end. Miraculously, no one did hit him. He tried to stand, but pain shot through his chest. He fell to the track, trying to suck air into his starved lungs. Ambulance attendants rushed to his side. They knelt to talk to him, but he couldn't speak. It felt as though he would never breathe again. The attendants carefully removed his helmet and chest protector, and loosened his racing pants. They supported him gently while his breath came back in ragged gasps. He felt a little better except for the sharp pain in his chest. When he opened his eyes, anxious faces peered down at him through a thin haze.

As his vision cleared, he saw Bill's concerned face and managed a slight smile.

"You alright, Buddy?" Bill asked

"I think so."

He tried to get up. The attendants gently pushed him back, strapped him onto a backboard and eased him onto a stretcher.

"Hey, you guys, I'm okay," Mike weakly protested.

"Right kid, right," one friendly attendant said. "We're just going to make sure by letting the doctors at the hospital check you out."

"But I can move everything," he said. As he started to move his left arm, pain shot through his left side. Mike said nothing but it showed on his face. The attendant saw it.

"Don't worry kid, probably just a bruised rib. No sweat," he said as they lifted Mike and moved toward the ambulance.

Mike was a favorite at the local motocross tracks in central New York and a concerned crowd had gathered along the fence nearby. Mike waved at them with his right hand as they lifted him into the ambulance. The crowd applauded and called out encouragement. Bill climbed into the jump seat beside Mike, "You sure impressed the crowd with that one, fella."

"I may have impressed the crowd, but I don't think I impressed those Honda reps."

"That's for sure, but like everyone says, there's always next year."

"Yeah." Mike retreated into his own thoughts.

Sorrow and questions soared through his mind. He was positive he could have won the race - nobody was near at the start. Why didn't I spot that rock when I was checking the track before the race? I'm not sure which is worse, the pain in my side, or losing a factory ride. No nationals next year he thought glumly.

Mike knew he'd already won the District motocross championship because of the points accumulated for the season, but this did not overcome his disappointment. This had been the year to accomplish his goal of factory sponsorship. Now, in the ambulance speeding to the hospital he knew he had failed. All his plans of running the southern circuit during the winter months were wiped out in one stupid crash. He was way out ahead at the start. He could have backed off just a bit. Not spotting that rock in the pre-race track inspection was inexcusable. What would those reps think? Not only had he been reckless they'd think he was careless also.

He shifted his weight on the stretcher and winced at the pain in his side. The thoughts of missing the chance to ride on a factory team faded as he worried if he would ever ride again. The pain became more intense and he had trouble breathing.

Bill noticed Mike's discomfort, reached over and gently squeezed his arm. "Take it easy, Mike. We're almost to the hospital."

CHAPTER TWO

The ambulance swung into the emergency entrance. Mike was wheeled inside and transferred to an examining table. A waiting doctor checked him and ordered x-rays.

As they wheeled Mike into x-ray, the friendly ambulance attendant walked alongside. "We'll wait a few minutes to see if they keep you here, Mike. If you're okay, we'll give you a lift back to the track."

"Thanks. I'd rather ride with you guys than on an elevator going upstairs to the operating room."

The attendant laughed as they wheeled into the x-ray room.

Fifteen minutes later, Mike was back in the examining room waiting for the results. Mike and Bill waited. anxiously, not speaking.

Motocross Mike

It was Mike who broke the silence. "Bill, we better call Mom as soon as we know anything. If she hears about this from someone else, we're in big trouble."

Bill made a face. "I'd rather go back and take your crash for you. But you're right. There's a pay phone in the hall. You better talk to her first. She won't be happy until she hears your voice."

"She's already sour on my racing. This isn't going to help. If Dad was alive I know I'd be doing the same thing. It's what he'd want me to do. She says she loved him, yet when I do the things that I know he'd want me to, she's upset."

"Don't be too hard on her, Mike. Seeing you race brings back some really bad memories."

"I know she loved Dad a lot and that causes her a lot of worry about my racing but jeez, I've hardly been scratched until now"

Bill turned to see the doctor returning with x-rays in hand. "Here's the doctor. Let's take one thing at a time, kid."

"Well, Mike", the doctor said cheerfully, "I think you're going to live, but it's going to be awfully tough for you to take a deep breath for a few days. All we can see is one fractured rib, one cracked rib and a cracked collarbone."

Mike and Bill both smiled with relief. They were familiar with motorcycle injuries and these were fairly common and not considered real bad. Some riders would be back in the saddle in a

Charles Loomis

few weeks. Fortunately for Mike, the season was over. He could rest.

The doctor shook his head as he saw Mike and Bill smile. "You motocross racers are nuts. Every time I tell one of you that you've cracked or broken a rib or a collarbone you act like I'm telling you a joke.

"Look, Mike, I'm serious," he went on, "I know you want to race again, so you take care of yourself. Wear this brace for a couple of weeks and keep your arm in this sling for at least a week or until the collarbone feels better. You can go to school but no heavy exercise, lifting weights or anything like that for at least three weeks. And then go real easy."

He handed Mike an orange plastic container. "These pills will help you sleep for the next three or four days. After that, you won't need them. But you'd better check with your doctor back home as soon as you can."

Mike grimaced as he sat up and the doctor showed him how to use the brace and sling. The doctor walked them to the door where the ambulance was still waiting. Mike moved slowly as badly bruised and strained muscles tightened up on him. He paused at the telephone in the hallway. "Let's call her on the way home, Bill, I don't feel like talking just yet."

Bill gave him an understanding nod. "Okay, no problem," he said.

"Don't worry, Mike," the doctor said. "You're going to be pretty stiff for a couple of days, but you'll be fine before you know it. You must have taken quite a spill."

"So they tell me," Mike replied. "I don't remember much about it."

"Well, good luck." The doctor waved and turned away.

Back at the track, Mike's friends and some of the other riders were waiting.

"How much damage, Mike?" one asked.

"To me or the bike?" Mike smiled.

"To you, clown, we've already seen your bike. Good luck."

"That bad, eh?" Bill said as they elbowed their way through the crowd gathered around his van.

There, leaning against the van, was Mike's broken motorcycle.

"Oh, no," Mike groaned as they got a look at it.

The handlebars and frame were broken and bent. The swing arm was twisted. The back wheel hung from it and lay on the ground. Everything was a mess - clutch, brake and shift levers broken or hanging loose. The stress on the engine when it flipped had cracked the cases and oil seeped out in a dark stain.

Mike shuddered as he gazed at his broken machine. He was lucky.

"Well," said Bill interrupting his thoughts, "We might as well pack up and hit the road. We're done for the day and I imagine a nice hot bath would feel good right now. We've got to call your mom too."

"Yeah, Bill," Mike replied, "I'm really beginning to stiffen up."

"Mike," a friend called, "you sit down, we'll help Bill load the van."

"Thanks, guys, I'd appreciate that." Mike settled into the nearest lawn chair.

The next 250 moto was just starting and Mike watched longingly as the riders went off the line. "They all should know where that rock is now." he thought.

All at once, Mike spotted the two Honda representatives approaching across the parking lot.

"Hi, Mike, I'm Jim Hawkins and this is Hugh Black."

Mike stood up stiffly and grasped the out-stretched hand.

"Stay in the chair, Mike," Hugh Black said as he shook Mike's hand. "We're both ex-motocross riders, so we know how you feel right now. Sounds like you've got a bit of healing to do."

"Ribs and collarbone, that's all. No sweat."

"That was some spill," Jim, said, "I don't think I've ever had one that bad. Not one I can remember, anyway."

Motocross Mike

"It was stupidity on my part. I should have spotted that rock when I walked the track before the race."

"Well, you can't win them all. But I understand that's just about what you've been doing this year."

"Yeah, I had a good year. The bike has been running good and Bill is probably the best mechanic a guy could have."

"You know we came here to watch you run today, don't you, Mike?" asked Hugh.

"Yeah," Mike smiled. "You sure picked the wrong day for me."

Hugh continued, "Don't worry about it. Everybody has a bad day now and then. There's always next year. Besides, we understand you've got one more year in high school. You finish that, get another season in and maybe we'll see you next year."

Hugh turned to Jim, "Well, what do you say, Jim? We better hit the road."

Mike rose to say good-bye. "Okay Mr. Hawkins, Mr. Black, nice to see you. I'll see if I can give you a better performance next time you come out."

Bill came around the van. "Hey Champ, ready to go when you are. Hugh, Jim. Nice to see you guys. We'll have a better show for you next time you come out.".

Mike made his way to the van, thanked his friends for helping Bill and they left for home.

Charles Loomis

"You hungry kid? Let's find a place to get a bite and you can call your mom."

"I'm not hungry. If I know mom and Janice they'll have something on the stove for us. But we'd better stop and call."

Bill pulled into a fast food restaurant and ordered a hamburger and soda while Mike dialed home. "Hi mom, now don't get nervous, I took a spill but I'm okay."

"Michael, you wouldn't be calling me if you were okay. Now tell me what happened. Where are you?"

"We're at a restaurant. We're on our way home." He heard his mother breathe a sigh of relief.

"Michael, I'm glad you're not in the hospital but tell me the truth. How bad are you hurt? You wouldn't be calling me for a little scratch."

"Well, I wanted you to hear about it from me and not someone who left early or something. I went over the bars on the start of the first moto. I banged my ribs a little."

"What's a little?"

"One's broken but the other is just bruised."

"Oh God! Michael, when are you going to give up this foolishness? Lord, you are your father's son. Did you see a doctor?"

"Yes."

"What did he say?"

"He said my ribs and my collarbone will heal up in no time at all."

"Collarbone! You didn't say anything about a collarbone. What about your collarbone?"

"It's only cracked, Mom. It's hardly even sore if I hold still. My ribs hurt, though."

"Thank God you're in one piece! Oh Michael, please come home. I'm going to call Dr. Phillips right away. He'll be at his office when you get here."

"Aw Mom, don't worry so much. I'm okay - really. This doctor was good. They took x-rays and everything."

"I don't care. I want you home now. I want to talk to you and to Bill, too."

"Aw, Mom."

"Michael, I want you home now!" she said sternly and hung up the phone.

Bill stopped chewing his hamburger as he watched Mike's face and heard his side of the conversation. "I have a feeling that we are in deep trouble, ol' Buddy."

"You got it. We better get going."

"Don't be too tough on her Mike, Moms worry a lot and your Mom has good reason. Losing your Dad in that race at the Barkerville Raceway Half Mile doesn't help her attitude any

Charles Loomis

either. Want the rest of this?" Bill said as he offered the uneaten half of his burger to Mike and climbed back behind the wheel.

"Thanks Bill. Jeez, how can she get so upset over a couple of ribs and a collarbone?"

"She always expects the worse, Mike, and you can't blame her after your father died."

On the way, Bill attempted some small talk, but his attempts met with silence. Mike sat quietly, trying to hold back the tears. His body ached, but his heart ached more. There's always next year they'd said. But Mike wanted it this year. He was almost positive, the reps would have offered him a contract if he had shown them a good ride.

"I've got to start using my brain more and my throttle less. I had it right in the palm of my hand, Bill, and I blew it," he said in a quaking voice, tears of disappointment rolling down his cheeks.

"I know, kid, I know. Don't worry, some day they'll come crawling to get you to ride for them."

CHAPTER THREE

Mike was depressed. It was his senior year - school had started - but he just wouldn't go. His mother knew that his injuries weren't bad enough to keep him home, yet each time she brought up the subject of school he began complaining about his aches and pains. He spent his days since the crash moping about the house.

All Mike could think of was motocross and how much he loved the sport. The winter months meant no racing. If he'd gotten the factory ride, he could have ridden the winter series in Florida or California. School could wait. He could finish that anytime.

Motocross was a different story. It couldn't and wouldn't wait. Mike knew that very few riders still rode past their late twenties. It was a tough, demanding sport, said to be second only to soccer in the need for strength and stamina. The tremendous demands on the body "washed out" most riders by the time they were thirty.

Charles Loomis

Mike figured he had maybe ten good years left, and he wanted to take advantage of every possible minute. If he couldn't ride, he didn't want to do anything.

Even Chub, Mike's best friend and favorite trail riding partner was exasperated with him. Chub got his nickname from the few extra pounds he carried around. They were due to Chub's enormous appetite. But the few extra pounds made very little difference in the way Chub could handle a motorcycle. He could wheelie across a field as far as he had room and as long as he wanted. And on a trail ride through the woods, he appeared to almost fly.

Standing up on the pegs, bent slightly over the handlebars, weight back with arms loose and relaxed Chub looked like the greatest rider in the world. Using body english and carefully shifting his weight, he could ride the tightest sections with hardly any change in speed. His hands flicked the clutch, throttle, and front brake skillfully as his foot would find the proper gear for the terrain he was on without ever missing a shift.

While Mike's dream was to become a professional motocross racer, Chub's ambition was to qualify for the International Six Days Enduro some day. For now, however, he was content to run local cross-country events.

Before the accident, Mike had worked for Bill in the bike shop after school and on weekends. Chub decided to come up

Motocross Mike

with a plan to snap his friend out of his depression and he told Bill Maslak about it. Bill agreed that the plan was a good one and Chub got busy.

"Hey, guess what, hot shot?" Chub said to Mike one day during their daily after school visits. "Bill gave me your job until your brittle bones heal."

"Oh, that's good," Mike answered without enthusiasm. "I'm sure Bill could use the help. It's a good deal for you. You can use the money to race in the Fall Enduro season."

"Not to mention," Chub continued, "I can wrench just as good as you with my eyes closed."

That upset Mike just a bit.

"Rebuilding an engine is a bit different than changing a spark plug out in the woods, klutz." Mike replied.

"I learn fast, brittle bones. You're going to be lucky you have a job if you ever get your body back together."

"You'll find out whose body needs putting back together when I get feeling better, jelly belly."

Chub thought he had hit just the right nerve. He jumped into his favorite fighting pose in anticipation of the make-believe fight he thought would follow. But Mike simply settled deeper into his chair and gazed back at the cartoons on television.

Chub shrugged and sat back down.

Charles Loomis

Ann Porter, Mike's mother, stood in the hall, smiling a little at Chub's attempt to shake Mike out of his blues.. Though disappointed at his lack of success, she knew Chub wasn't finished yet.

About a week later Mike, was again watching television when he heard a familiar noise behind the house. From the sound of things, Chub was using the motocross practice track they'd set up behind his house. The two of them spent many hours racing each other around it.

Mike moved to the window and saw his friend, making his way around the track on a motocross bike. He noticed the absence of a headlight and taillight. That can't be Chub's bike, he thought. As a matter of fact, it looks like mine.

It was a warm fall day and Mike pushed the screen door open. He stood on the patio and watched Chub make his way around the track on the bike that looked and sounded like his. Finally, Chub rode off the track and down to where Mike stood.

Mike couldn't believe his eyes. It was his old bike! Chub grinned, revving the engine..

"So I'm a lousy mechanic, eh?" he said. "You don't know what I had to go through to get this mashed beast back on the track again. But when you're an enduro rider, you can make anything run if you really want to."

Motocross Mike

Mike stared at his old bike for a moment. He couldn't believe it was running again. He circled it carefully as Chub watched him, a smug smile on his face.

"But how did you--," Mike began, then stopped. "It really runs?"

"Well, I wouldn't say that it runs as good as it used to," Chub replied. "But all things considered, it's not that bad. It has a tendency not to want to go in a perfectly straight line, but it goes good enough to have a little fun. I don't think it will ever race again, though. Want to take it for a little spin?"

"Let me take it up the path and back." Mike said. "I don't think I can manage it around the track. You know - with my collar bone and all."

Chub concealed his delight. His plan was working. "Sure, take my helmet," he said as he got off the bike and held it as Mike got on.

With a toss of his head Mike's long dark hair lay back as he pulled Chub's helmet on. His blue eyes lit up as a grin spread over his face and he adjusted Chub's goggles over his eyes.

Mike kicked the bike to life. He shifted down into low gear and slowly made his way up the path.

Chub watched his friend with a secret pride. He knew that taking Mike's job and now his bike had been more than Mike could stand. He and Bill had worked hard to get Mike's smashed

Charles Loomis

up bike running. They bent, pried and welded Mike's frame back into somewhere near rideable shape. They had taken used parts off old bikes and some that were lying around the shop and nursed the heap back to life. It wasn't the best but it was serving its purpose. Mike was riding again.

When he got to the track, Mike couldn't resist the temptation . He turned right on to the track and before he knew it, he was bounding along the whoopdiedoos. He was going slow, but the important thing was that he was doing it.

"Wow, Chub was right, this thing doesn't know where it wants to go," he thought as he put his foot down and plowed heavily into a turn. On the back straight, he fought to keep it in a straight line. Chub wasn't kidding when he said it was a little difficult to ride. Mike took two easy laps until he began to feel the ache of his weakened, unused muscles.

At the same time he saw his angry mother making her way up the pathway.

"Michael," she called irritably as he rode down to where she was standing. She always called him Michael when she was angry with him. "If you're too sick to go to school, you're too sick to ride that thing."

"It's okay Mom, I wasn't going very fast. I was going to quit now, anyway. I'm too sore to go any further. Wow, am I out of shape!."

Motocross Mike

Mike's mom didn't know whether to be disappointed or relieved. Part of her had been secretly hoping Chub's plan would fail. She looked at Mike and sighed. If only he'd go back to school and on to college. Forget about racing. Every time she saw Mike on a motorcycle brought back visions of the terrible racing accident that had killed Mike's dad, Mike Sr.

He'd been racing partners with Bill Maslak as well as in the motorcycle shop. Both professional flat track racers, they'd been very successful at both endeavors. Ann Porter knew that equipment and tracks were much safer now and serious injuries to motocross racers were actually quite rare. But, she could never get the memories of Mike Senior's death out of her mind.

Chub followed Mrs. Porter up the path. He took the bike from Mike as he got off. "Well, what do you think?"

"It'll never win a national, but it's good enough to have some fun with." Mike replied.

"I've got to get back to the shop before it gets dark." He swung away from Mike and his mother. Chub was very happy. Mike's mother was not.

Mike and his mother walked slowly down the path to the house. "I can tell you liked your little ride," she said, "and I can also see that you're doing a lot of thinking. Are you thinking about riding again?"

"Maybe," Mike answered. They continued back to the house in silence.

Mike didn't sleep too well that night. He tossed and turned as he thought about riding and how he had let himself get out of shape over the past few weeks. I think I'll go to school tomorrow, he thought as he drifted off to sleep.Maybe it's time.

His dreams, however, were always the same. He would be at the start line, ready to roar off in a race against some of the greatest riders in the world. Only his bike would stall as the gate dropped and the pack pulled away from him to disappear in the distance as he frantically tried to re-start.

Sometimes, the dreams changed a little, but their message was the same. He would get a good start, but one by one the other bikes would pass him as his bike mysteriously lost power. Full throttle, yet some of the slowest local riders would drift by him, grinningly wickedly. In other dreams, his mother would jump out in front of him waving him to stop as other riders passed.

He would awaken from these nightmares damp with perspiration, his heart full of dread and anger. Relieved that he had only been dreaming, he would fall back into a restless sleep.

The dreams came this night also, but when he awoke his anxiety left him quickly. For the first time in weeks, he could smile at his fright.

Motocross Mike

"I'm Mike Porter," he thought. " I'm the fastest rider in district three and next year I'm going to go even faster."

CHAPTER FOUR

The next morning , Mike made his way down the driveway to meet the school bus. He knew there would be some embarrassing questions from his friends about where he had been since school had started three weeks before. He didn't care, however, because now his mind was on the track team and getting into shape. Running three to five times a week was part of his training routine for motocross all year long and now he was the best long distance runner on the Westville High School track team and one of the best in the whole league.

He also had a passion for wrestling and was on the varsity team. One on one, or individual sports seemed to attract him more than team sports such as football, baseball and basketball.

Both running and wrestling were excellent conditioners for motocross. Running built up his endurance and leg muscles, while wrestling strengthened the upper chest, back and arm muscles so necessary for hanging on to a bike over a rough motocross course.

As he'd expected, his friends kidded him about his absence from school.

"I thought motocross riders were supposed to be tough," one said.

"Finally decided to come down from the mountain and join us peasants, huh Mike?" said another.

Mike smiled at the friendly teasing. His friends laughed as he faked a pronounced limp and groaned as if in extreme pain as he made his way back to the seat on the school bus that Chub had saved for him.

"Okay, man, nice to have you back," Chub said as he whacked Mike on the knee. "It's going to be nice to have someone to talk to who knows something about bikes instead of the rest of the animals in this zoo transporter."

"Don't forget, you're part of this cargo, Chub," Andy Hill answered with a laugh. "The way you eat, it puts you in the elephant class."

Chub leaned way back, patted his ample stomach and said very seriously, "I'm predicting a world-wide famine and I figure as long as I keep this, I'll be the last one to go."

The three boys laughed as the bus pulled up in front of the school and they got off.

Mike pulled Chub aside. "I just want to say thanks, old pal. You got me going again. I talked with Mom last night and she said this whole plan was your idea.."

Chub's face turned beet red. He recovered quickly and his look of embarrassment was soon replaced by a look of mischief. "Yeah, it was my idea. But you know I kind of like the job, I don't think I'll give that back."

Mike laughed as he faked a punch to Chub's mid section. "Some friend," he said.

Before long, Mike started to run seriously again and soon he was back on the track team. His coach was glad to see him back. Before the accident. Mike had been an anchor on the cross country team He was now running comfortably and after a couple of weeks came in among the leaders for his team.

Getting back into shape improved Mike's mental attitude also. He slept better and his bad dreams disappeared as he began to think more positively about the new motocross season.

One night when he got home, he got a call from Bill. "You want to start back to work?" Bill asked.

"Sure!" Mike answered excitedly. "But what about Chub?"

"Chub's Dad needs him on the farm."

Mike didn't exactly believe this, but he wasn't about to argue.

"Come in tomorrow after school and we'll set up a schedule for you." Bill told him. And hung up.

The next day, Bill showed Mike the brochures for the new motocross bikes.

"Wow, twelve inches of travel on each end," Bill exclaimed, as they read the brochure. "You could take the big bumps pretty fast with that."

"Yeah, and I'll need a stepladder to get on the thing too," Mike replied. "Are you sure you still want to sponsor me after that idiot crash this fall?"

"Sure, why not?" was Bill's cheerful reply. "You know I like to go to the races as much as you do. It gives me a good excuse. Besides, you're the fastest rider in the district. That's good advertising for the shop." Bill's eyes twinkled with excitement.

"I placed the order for two new CR's this morning. If you're going to start running the nationals next year you're going to need a practice bike, right? So think of one as a loaner from your sponsor. The other is an early graduation present."

For a moment, Mike was too awed to speak. He looked at his older friend. "Bill, you're the greatest. Thanks--thanks a lot. You won't regret it. I promise you that.."

"My pleasure, Mike," Bill replied. "Next season is going to be your best yet. I really think you're going to make pro and that's going to make me happy too. You've got the skill, the drive and the experience. I know you can do it."

After the shop closed at nine that evening, Mike ran the short distance to Chub's house. He was bursting with excitement and wanted to share the good news with his friend.

"Guess what?" he said to his friend.

"Whaddya mean, guess what?" Chub said sleepily. After a hard day's work on the family farm, he usually fell asleep in front of the TV or over his homework. He wasn't in any mood for guessing games at nine-thirty at night.

"I'm definitely riding for Bill next spring." Mike said as he danced around Chub poking him playfully. He ordered two new CR250's for me this morning. They should be here in about a month."

"Wow, you're even getting a practice bike. Big time, really big time. Wow," he said, again ducking Mike's punches. "Those are some motocross bikes - twelve inches of travel front and rear, all the power you need, light. Wow!"

Mike started to laugh as Chub's enthusiasm started to show through. "I'm going to show every rider in District Three the fastest line around every track," he said.

"Yeah hotshot," Chub said. "You better stay in good shape because a new bunch of riders move up to expert every year. I heard that Ackley is moving up to the 250cc class. He's fast and tough and rumor has it he wants your hide."

"It's going to be pretty tough to take my skin off when he's a couple of hundred yards behind me, old buddy, because that's how far ahead of him I'll be," Mike announced, shooting a fast left to Chub's stomach. "Pros, watch out because here I come."

Chub flinched from Mike's left to his stomach and decided that was enough. He got Mike in a headlock and the two friends crashed to the floor laughing.

"Cut it out," Chub's father yelled from the next room. "Crazy kids, " he muttered. "Go wrestle on the front lawn if you have to, but not in the house."

Mike and Chub settled on the stairs in the front hall. They jabbered about the changes in the new bikes and the season ahead until Mike realized it was close to eleven o'clock.

"Mom's going to be worried," he said. "I better get going."

"Okay, see you tomorrow, pal. Man, I can't wait to take a spin on those babies. Let me know as soon as they come in and we'll go over them together."

"Good enough," Mike said as he hurried down the front steps and turned towards the lights on his front porch. "See ya, buddy."

CHAPTER FIVE

Ann Porter sat watching television and waited for her son to come home. She knew why he was late. She knew that he was at Chub's discussing the new bikes that had been ordered for him. She'd continued the partnership with Bill Maslak in the motorcycle shop after Mike's father was killed, and was the bookkeeper and office manager in a now thriving business.

She knew about Mike's motorcycles because she had been posting invoices that morning and had come across the special orders for the new CR's. Usually she and Bill discussed new bike orders and always discussed which models and what quantity of each to order. A special order such as this meant only one thing - new bikes for Mike.

As always, the thought of Mike's racing brought back the awful memories of the day Mike's father was killed. Ann hoped that after her son's crash, his attention would turn toward college and a career other than motorcycling. She was his mother--she couldn't help but worry about it.

Ann had confronted Bill with a copy of the invoice that morning.

"These bikes are for Mike aren't they?" she'd asked.

Bill had shrugged uncomfortably. "Yeah, " he admitted. "I phoned the order in this morning. They were real happy to hear that Mike was going to continue to race. They like him."

"They like anyone who wins for them." Ann had answered darkly. "Bill, you know I appreciate everything you've done for Mike since his father died. But he's my son! Don't you think you could have discussed it with me first?"

Bill sighed. "I wanted it to be a surprise. Ann," he went on. "It's not like I'm sending the kid off to war. Come on, will ya? It's what he wants to do more than anything else in the world. He can go to college later. If you talk him out of racing now, he's going to regret it all his life. He's good, you know it, and so do I. So does he."

"His father was good too, where is he now?"

"Racing is different today. You know that. Helmets are better, bikes are safer, and tracks are safer. Besides, this is motocross, not flat track. His father was fast and good, but the guys who win today are not necessarily the fastest. They're the ones in the best condition, strong enough to hold on over the rough stuff. That's

Mike - he's strong and tough. It's what he trains for every day. How can you take it all away from him?"

"Maybe I could if I had some help from you." With that, she had turned away and headed back to the office, slamming the door behind her.

Now, Ann Porter turned off the television as she heard Mike come in the front door.

He threw off his jacket and kicked his sneakers into the hall closet. "Hi Mom," he called cheerfully. "Sorry I'm late."

She couldn't help but smile as she looked at him. She might not want to admit it, but Mike hadn't looked this happy in weeks. "That's alright," she replied. " I knew you and Chub had a lot to talk about."

Mike stared at her. "You know about the new bikes?"

"Of course silly, I post all the invoices don't I?"

"You're not mad?"

"Well, you know how I feel about your racing. I don't exactly feel like going out to celebrate, if that's what you mean."

"Mom?"

"Yes dear, what is it?"

"Do you think Dad would be proud of how well I race?"

Mrs. Porter wrapped her arms around Mike and hugged him, holding back her tears. "Yes sweetheart, I think he'd be very proud."

CHAPTER SIX

That weekend, Mike and Chub were on their bikes once again. Out in the woods near Chub's farm it was a perfect day for it. They'd spent hours flying two or three feet in the air off a frozen snowdrift, running, cresting and landing side by side on a hard-packed crust of snow. They couldn't have asked for a better surface. The crust was the result of two days of drizzling rain, followed by bitter cold.

A whole day of fun lay ahead of them. They could explore the hard-packed snowmobile trails around Chub's farm or wander the neighboring countryside. The snow crust was so hard that they could even swing off the trails if they wished, and search out new adventures.

That was how they'd found the snowdrift they were on right now. It was perfectly situated right at the top of a slight downhill slope. After a few test flights off the crest they were stretching out

Charles Loomis

their jumps or "getting some air" as motocross riders call it. Over and over, they wheelied off for a short distance to swing around again for another flight off the jump.

Then as Chub, who was heavier than Mike, landed off the crest, his bike broke through the hard packed crust--stopped dead and sent Chub sprawling over the handlebars.

Chub rolled and slid down the rest of the slope, finally coming to a stop. He was laughing loudly. Bundled up in two or three layers of clothing topped off by a snowmobile suit (and his helmet, of course), he was not hurt in the least.

Mike slowly rolled his bike to a stop near Chub. After seeing that he wasn't hurt Mike laughed along with him.

" You look like a big fat puppy-- playing in the snow." he chuckled.

"No more jumps, for me, buddy." Chub said as he restarted his bike, after freeing it from the snowbank. "I'm sticking to the snowmobile trails. Hey! Let's ride up a ways and see if we can get up that big hill on the Marshall place." Chub paused thoughtfully. On the other hand, we could go eat first. I'm hungry."

Mike grinned. Chub was always hungry. "It's only eleven o'clock!"

"Oh," Chub replied. "Jeez, it seems later than that."

Mike started off up the trail with Chub close behind. Mike's battered and patched motocross bike was running pretty good

Motocross Mike

and he picked up the pace a bit. Metal screws they had placed in the tires bit into the hard packed snowmobile trail. The two boys had spent the evening before screwing sheet metal screws into each knob on the tires. Five hundred screws per tire gave them excellent traction. Happy at the clear, cold morning and the sparkling snow, Mike lofted the front wheel into a wheelie.

When they reached the hill on the Marshall place, they paused at the base and peered up through the trees to make sure no snowmobiles were on their way down. The hill was two hundred yards long and steep, so there was very little room to get a run at it. It was difficult enough in the summer, but now, with the ruts and bumps the snowmobiles had made in their struggles to make it to the top, it was even tougher.

"Go!" Mike shouted as he kicked his bike down into second gear, popped the clutch and covered Chub with a shower of snow crystals.

"I'll get you for that." Chub shouted as he followed his friend.

But Mike didn't hear him; he was lost in his own world of hill and bike. The engine screamed as it hit top rpm's and he eased it up into third gear as he flew through the air off the first bump. Standing up on the pegs, he landed on the face of the next bump, almost bottoming out the rear suspension.

Charles Loomis

The front end came up, threatening to loop the bike over backwards, but Mike was in control. He backed off the throttle and prepared for the next jump. He hit it at full throttle, twisted the bike slightly to set up for the curve, and landed sideways--perfectly lined up for the turn.

Twisting the throttle wide open again, he roosted a shower of snow into the air, shifted into fourth and headed along a more level spot on the hill. He slid around an abrupt left-hand turn, dropped back down into third gear and started climbing again, bouncing and lurching his way to the top of the steep slope.

Whether to take the hill sitting on the seat or standing on the pegs was never a question in his mind. At the speed he was traveling, it would have been impossible to sit on the seat over the rough terrain. His legs and arms, together with the bike's suspension absorbed the rocking and bouncing. Any attempt to sit in those conditions would have catapulted him off the bike.

At the top, Mike paused to wait for Chub. He didn't have to wait long. This was Chub's world. He was just as much at home on a woods trail as he was in his own backyard.

He slid to a stop next to his friend, a broad grin on his face. "Let's do it again," he said. Before Mike could say a word, Chub revved his bike, popped the clutch in low gear, leaned the bike down, and did a one-hundred and eighty degree turn in the middle

Motocross Mike

of the trail. He laughed as he watched Mike ducking the snow shower created by his spinning rear wheel.

"Gotcha," Chub yelled as he bounced off down the trail.

Mike set off to catch his friend in a wild ride down the steep slope. He caught Chub on the corner. Chub went a little wide and Mike, seeing his chance, stuck his right leg out almost in front of the front wheel, leaned his bike down so that the right handlebar almost touched the snow on the inside of the curve and gassed out. He passed Chub and could hear him yelling in frustration as he went by.

Mike wheelied along the straight section to the slight left hand curve. He slid through it and hit the final, bumpy downhill section. He stood up on the pegs, moved back over the rear wheel, and plunged into the steepest part of the downhill without hesitation. Anyone watching the bouncing, swerving bike and rider would have sworn he was headed for disaster.

But Mike was completely relaxed on the bouncing, bucking machine. His arms and legs moved in harmony, absorbing the shocks as the bike leaped down, up and over the mounds of snow.

At the bottom of the hill, he waited until Chub pulled up beside him. "Nice practice," he said with a grin. "Let's go back up, take the trail back to your house, and find something to eat," Chub begged. "My stomach is growling like a freight train."

Charles Loomis

The trails were perfect - not too much ice. They had been used enough by snowmobiles to be firmly packed and widened. It was a beautiful day. A perfect day to ride the trails. The sun remained bright and warm while the air stayed crisp and cold.

On hard packed trails with conditions like this, they could ride faster than any snowmobiles they might meet, but they always pulled over. Some snowmobiles had never seen a motorcycle on the trails in the winter and their riders were always very interested in the young men and their machines.

Mike and Chub answered their questions as well as they could and were always friendly and polite. It was their way of making sure they would continue to be welcome in this winter setting.

Their odometers read forty-two miles.

"Not bad for the first time out, eh Chub?" Mike inquired of his friend.

"Ah, that was nothing," Chub answered, as he was reached down to shut off the gas on his bike. "We were out for three hours. Let's see - forty-two miles divided by three is fourteen miles an hour. That's all we averaged, just fourteen miles an hour. If I was in an enduro, I would have had to ride twenty-four miles an hour. I would've had to do what we did today in less than two hours."

Chub always minimized every ride. It was never too hard or too long, never just right. Something always could have been better about it - his style, his speed, his timing. That was probably

Motocross Mike

what made him such a good trail rider. He analyzed everything he did. It used to irritate Mike until he realized that when it came to his motocross riding, he did the same thing.

"Yeah, I guess you're right," Mike replied. "But it was sure a good ride." He started to laugh. "I couldn't believe it when you wiped out. You should have seen yourself rolling and sliding along in the snow."

Mike pulled off his helmet and goggles. His blue eyes were sparkling from the excitement and the fun of the great ride they had just had. He smoothed back his long dark hair. He was slender, and would have looked skinny if it wasn't for his broad shoulders and muscular neck.

He was a firm believer in conditioning. He read everything he could get his hands on that had anything to do with professional motocross racing and the riders. All he read pointed to one thing - conditioning. He had activities planned for every season and in between. He jogged, lifted weights in his cellar and had a daily routine of exercise. His favorite conditioner, however, was trail riding with Chub.

Mike's mother welcomed the boys at the door as they were kicking the snow from their boots. Despite her anxiety about Mike's racing she was proud of her son's achievements.

"How was the ride boys?" Mrs. Porter asked as she led them into the kitchen.

"It was perfect Mom," Mike replied. "I've never seen winter riding so good. We're going back out this afternoon."

"How about you Chub, did you enjoy yourself?"

"Oh yeah, it was good," Chub said as he eyed the stove where a big kettle of homemade soup was bubbling. "Uh, is that soup for us, Mrs. Porter?"

"Why sure Chub. You guys go wash up and I'll put some soup and sandwiches out for us."

Chub brightened and practically knocked Mike over getting to the bathroom sink.

The two friends playfully elbowed each other at the sink as they washed their hands and glowing faces.

"Hey Mom," Mike shouted. "If Chub gets out of here before I do, make sure you don't put anything on the table until I get there - he'll eat it all up."

"Michael, that's no way to treat a guest," Mrs. Porter protested.

"This is no guest, this is an eating machine," Mike said as he unsuccessfully dodged a glob of soapsuds that Chub had aimed at his face.

Chub came out of the bathroom, hitching up his pants over the slight paunch of his stomach and eyed the plate of sandwiches and bowls of hot soup.

Motocross Mike

"His bad manners don't bother me none, Mrs. Porter," Chub said with a smile. "He's just jealous because he's skinny and I got a he-man physique."

Mrs. Porter smiled as Chub flexed his muscles in the classic strong man pose.

The boys ate well. They were both hungry. The brisk winter air and the morning workout on the bikes had given them both good appetites.

Mrs. Porter smiled as she watched the two friends dig in. The boys were lucky to get along so well. She couldn't remember a serious disagreement between them since they were toddlers arguing over a toy car or motorcycle in the sand box behind the house

Above all, they helped each other. More than once, they had re-built a blown engine the night before a race so that one of them could ride the next day. Mike went to enduros with Chub and ran the gas stops for him when he didn't have a motocross race to go to. Chub, on the other hand, was one of Mike's loudest supporters at motocross races when he had no enduro to go to himself.

"Gee, Mrs. Porter, that was delicious. Thanks for the great lunch." Chub said leaning back with a satisfied look on his face.

"That's quite alright Chub, I'm glad you enjoyed it."

"Where'll we go this afternoon?" Mike asked.

Charles Loomis

"Let's take a ride over to the shop and check the screws in the tires to see how they're holding up," Chub replied.

"Good idea, let's go. Bye Mom, see you later."

"Hold it you guys. I cooked, you clean up. It's the maids day off."

"Oh sure Mom - sorry. We'll have this mess cleaned up in just a minute."

Mike and Chub pitched into the clean up and were soon on their way.

"Bye Mom," Mike called. "We're going to take a ride over to Bill's and check the bikes out and then take another ride this afternoon."

"Okay boys, have fun and be careful," Mike's mother answered from the living room.

CHAPTER SEVEN

Mike and Chub rode their bikes over to the motorcycle shop. The shop was closed on Sunday, but Mike had a key. They let themselves in, put their bikes up on stands and systematically checked them out.

It had been their first snow ride so they went over the bikes carefully, first checking the screws to make sure they were tight and none of them had worked out of the tires. The spokes were next. Each one had to be tightened a little bit at a time as they turned the wheel. It took four or five complete rotations until the tension was just right.

Chub removed the carburetor air box on his bike to make sure snow had not gotten inside when he fell. Meanwhile, Mike checked and tightened all the nuts and bolts on his own bike - especially those around the handlebars and front forks. A loose nut or bolt in that area could cause an unexpected fall. They

Charles Loomis

adjusted the drive chains, topped off their fuel tanks and were ready to go once more.

Bill Maslak stopped by to catch up on some paperwork. Always fun to be around, the boys especially enjoyed his company. It was great to hear him tell stories about "the good old days", as Bill called them. Sometimes he would get out the album full of racing pictures of himself and Mike's father.

Mike loved to hear stories about his father's and Bill's racing days. Opening the cycle shop had been a natural progression of their friendship. When Mike's father died, Bill had tried hard to be a second father to Mike. And while Mike knew he would never stop missing his Dad, he treasured Bill's friendship.

"Hey!" Bill called to them. "Don't you know that motorcycles were made to be put away in the winter time?" Bill smiled. "Pretty soon, you'll have everybody riding cycles in the snow. If that happens, I won't sell any snowmobiles in the winter and there won't be any trails for you guys to ride. You ever try to ride a motorcycle on the snow without a hard packed trail to ride on?"

Mike looked at Chub with a mischievous grin.. "Chub tried that this morning," he said and burst out laughing.

Bill caught on right away. "How was it Chub? Tough going?"

Chub tried hard to look serious. "I didn't fall," he protested. " I was just practicing in case of an emergency."

Motocross Mike

The three of them laughed together.

Bill sat down on a stool near the workbench.

"You know, Mike," he went on. "Back when your Dad and I were doing a lot of riding, they didn't have snowmobiles. I never knew how much fun winter riding could be until you talked me into it. If the cold doesn't get to you it's almost as much fun as dirt riding."

"Yeah," Mike agreed. "Some of the bumps out on the snowmobile trails make them as rough as a motocross track. You hit places where it feels like you're riding a hobby horse, but it's still a lot of fun."

"Are you going out this afternoon?" Bill asked.

"You bet. In fact we're on our way. Why don't you come with us?"

"Not today guys." Bill shook his head slowly. "As a matter of fact, I was thinking of taking a little nap after I finish this paperwork. You take off and let an old man get his rest," Bill said as he pressed the button to open the garage door to let them out. "I'll see you later."

Bill watched as the two boys cranked up their bikes and wheelied onto the trail He grinned. It did look like fun.

The afternoon was just as enjoyable as the morning had been. Several hours later, Mike and Chub returned to Mike's house, hungry and thoroughly tired.

Charles Loomis

"I'm so hungry I could eat a skunk," Chub said.

"Hey--" Mike replied. "I hope your mother has a good recipe for skunk."

Chub made a face, considering the possibility. Mike waved tiredly. as Chub gunned his bike, kicking up a plume of snow.

"See you tomorrow, Chub, " He called over the roar of the engine.

That night, Mike ate dinner with his mother and turned in early. He was beat and soon fell into a deep, sound sleep.

And he dreamed about nothing at all.

CHAPTER EIGHT

When weekend conditions were right, the two boys continued to ride their bikes. During the week Mike's time was consumed by track and wrestling. Now that his injuries were healed, his spirits were completely revived. Everything he did helped him work toward his goal to become a professional motocross racer. Every footrace and wrestling match he saw as another step closer to that goal.

His coaches were amazed and impressed with the effort he put forth and his excellent physical condition. His performance at track meets was excellent. He had strength and endurance, developed by years of motocross and he always placed high. Sometimes, he even won.

Deep down, Mike felt a need to do his best, not necessarily for the team, but for himself. He set goals and constantly tried to better them. He kept track of his times at track meets and after awhile, could almost predict his time in a race over a given distance. Before long, he was elected captain of the cross-country team.

When the snows whipped out of the west, everyone began the long, patient wait until the spring thaws. But Mike was ready to wrestle. All his running during the fall paid off for wrestling, too. He'd dropped ten pounds and was able to wrestle in the 130-pound class.

Though Mrs. Porter fretted and scolded at Mike to eat more, Mike stuck to his diet of boiled eggs, chicken, fish and vegetables to maintain his wrestling weight. "Don't worry, " he assured his mom. "When motocross season comes around I'll make up for it.

Come spring, I'll eat more than Chub," he promised.

"Motocross is all I hear about around here, "She pleaded. "Can't I hear some mention of college?"

"Oh Mom, I've got time for that. I can go to college anytime, but I can only ride motocross when I'm young."

And so the winter wore on. Chub shared Mike's enthusiasm for wrestling and wrestled at one hundred and eighty pounds. He struggled and puffed at workouts and agonized to maintain that weight. His main opponent wasn't a wrestler, though. It was food- -Chub's main enemy, and sometimes his good friend, too.

Motocross Mike

"I just inhale around food and I gain weight," was his constant complaint. But his friends knew better.

One Saturday in February, when Mike walked into work, Bill's hello was a bit more enthusiastic than usual. He had a grin on his face that just wouldn't quit.

"What's up?" Mike asked.

"Check the back room."

Mike pushed through the swinging doors into the shop area and let out a whoop of delight. Two unopened crates sat in the middle of the shop - his bikes had arrived at last.

"Wow, give me the bar and the hammer, I'll have these babies out of the crate before you know it," he said as he started for his toolbox. "No, wait! I'd better call Chub first. He'll want to see these. Bill, should I call Chub first or uncrate the bikes?"

He stared at his boss, completely flustered with excitement.

"Whoa there, fella," Bill laughed. "You're going to take those doors right off their hinges. Call Chub so he can come over and open them up for you. He can handle that, while you're behind the counter. Today's a working day, remember?"

"Ok, good idea," Mike dialed Chub's number.

Chub answered the phone on the first ring. Bill could tell from hearing Mike's end of the conversation that Chub was just as excited as they were. Mike hung up, laughing. "Guess what? He's coming right over."

Charles Loomis

Bill chuckled. "I figured."

Ten minutes later they heard the sound of Chub's bike screaming into the parking lot. Chub burst through the door and headed right for the shop area.

"Where are those babies?" He said. "Let me at them. We'll see if they're as good as everyone says they are."

Mike was excited, too, but he went about working on the snowmobiles that Bill had lined up for him. For the next couple of hours, Chub busied himself opening the crates holding the two CR250 racers. Now and then, Mike left his work to check out some special feature that Chub discovered. Chub laid out each part on the bench with care, as Mike struggled to complete his work.. It was the first time that Mike would have a practice bike and it was difficult for him to contain his excitement and enthusiasm.

Even though one of them was destined to become a practice bike neither one of them would be ridden until each bike had been completely broken down, inspected, checked and reassembled. So Chub worked steadily and with great care. Not one gear, nut, screw, or bolt would be left unchecked. First, he had to clean each part to remove the protective spray they put on at the factory. The first race was more than a month away. But this time nothing would be left to chance. There wouldn't be any foul-ups -

mechanical, physical or mental. This time, Mike would win. Chub wanted that as much as Mike did.

By the end of the day, Chub had one bike completely laid out on the workbench in the corner of the shop reserved for Mike's racing. Mike finished with his last customer and turned his energies to the bikes. Piece by piece, he started reassembling all the parts Chub had laid out.

After locking the front door, Bill joined them . "Pretty nice, huh?" he said as he examined some of the parts. "Good attention to detail; nice machining."

Mike grinned up at him gratefully. "Really nice, Bill. The best!"

CHAPTER NINE

Spring came in fast. The sunshine warmed the earth and leaves began to appear on the bare trees. When he ran in the mornings, Mike saw the first robins and welcomed the fact that he was able to shed some of the layers of clothing he had run in all winter long.

Mike was happy. He felt he had never been in better shape and looked forward to the first race at the Royal Mountain motocross track. It was a fun time for him. He was busy and the days passed quickly. The snowmobile customers disappeared from the shop as the weather warmed and the motorcycle customers drifted back in. The new models were in and he and Bill had a great time showing off new features to the eager customers. Everything was going just fine. Mike found himself looking forward to rolling out of bed each morning.

Finally, the day arrived for his first race of the season.

Motocross Mike

Mike and Bill had gotten up and were on the road at seven o'clock in the morning for the hour trip to Royal Mountain They'd packed the van the night before with the two bikes, spare parts, tires, tubes, gas and a heavy toolbox crammed with everything they needed. They always carried the practice bike in case of a major break down. They might need a part they hadn't packed or even a complete engine.

Mike was excited. He kept up a steady stream of chatter with Bill as he drove the van through the early morning sunrise.

"It's going to be an interesting day, Bill."

"Yep, by the end of the day we'll find out who has been working out and taking care of themselves and who has been just laying around all winter long."

"And who has the best mechanic!" Mike added, "I think I've got them licked hands down in that area."

"Thanks, Mike. If I was a betting man, I think I know who I'd put my money on today."

"I know what you're thinking, Bill. But don't count your chickens before they hatch. There's some good riders coming out of amateur this year and some of the better riders from the 125cc class are moving to the 250 class.

It was eight o'clock on a Sunday morning when Bill and Mike pulled into Royal Mountain. The American Motorcyclist Association divided the country up into districts and each district

Charles Loomis

held a series of races. Mike raced in district three. A rider's number is awarded in accordance to the riders' finish the previous season. Since Mike had won the championship in District Three in the 250cc. Class he carried the number "1" plate in that class. The number "2" plate was assigned to the second place rider and so on down the line. Once in a while a rider had his favorite "good luck" number and he stuck with it regardless of what place he finished.

Mike peered through the windows at the crowded parking lot. "Like they say, it ain't going to be easy."

"What did Chub say about Walter Ackley?" Bill replied. "I heard you talking about him a while ago."

"He moved up here from District 32. They say he's good." Mike answered.

"Does he train? Has he got a good bike?"

"He's good, and for some reason he doesn't like me very much. I don't know why - I never did anything to him."

"Well, Mike, jealousy is a funny thing. When you win as much as you have, you're going to have enemies. People are funny sometimes. My old Grand Pop always said, 'nobody kicks a dog that's just lying around in the sun.' He probably doesn't like you just because you're good."

Motocross Mike

"Bill, I don't think I'm going to worry about it today, I'm just going to do the best I can. If anyone beats me then that's the way it goes. I'll just have to train a little harder."

Mike knew the bike would be all right. They had spent the previous night going over it inch by inch. Wheels, frame, engine, controls, everything had received the closest attention that any motorcycle mechanic could give.

He'd ridden the new bike until he felt it was completely broken in. He'd kept checking nuts and bolts to make sure he knew which ones to keep an eye on and which ones he could seal with "Loctite" to make sure they never loosened. Bill had then fine-tuned it as only Bill could do.

The afternoon before, Mike had practically stripped the bike, making sure that everything would be right. He had removed the seat, side panels, gas tank and wheels. He hand wiped the frame and engine components, checking every part and section to make sure nothing was loose, broken or starting to break. By the time he finished prepping, his hands would pass over practically every exterior part and surface on the bike.

Carefully, he'd re-checked the controls and cables to make sure that they would not fail. Bill had been busy with the shop. But even if he had the time, he rarely offered Mike much help in pre-race prep. It was a ritual that he and Mike both felt should be the rider's responsibility. Mike liked the handlebars tilted in a certain

Charles Loomis

way. He liked the controls set at just the right angle and tension. And while they might discuss some of the prepping procedures on the way to the race, almost always Bill would find that Mike had thought of everything.

He'd gone over the wheels-- checked the spokes and tightened them where necessary. The disk brakes had been completely disassembled and checked and the wheel bearings were greased. The tires and tubes were checked for dirt, punctures and abrasions. The tires were inflated to the proper amount, then the wheels were re-mounted back onto the bike.

He examined the carburetor carefully. The slightest bit of dirt there would mean a lost race. He cleaned the air filter in solvent, washed it and wrung it out carefully. After it had dried, he oiled it and greased the area where it seated against the air box and secured it. As part of the maintenance of the carburetor, he removed the float bowl to make sure no dirt or water had collected there.

Mike gave all the suspension components a once-over both front and rear. He checked carefully for oil leaks or loose or worn parts. And finally, he greased and oiled all necessary parts, changed the transmission oil and wire-brushed and oiled the chain.

"Yeah," he thought now. "The bike's ready. That's for sure," he thought, "But am I?"

"Hey hotshot, what's shakin'?"

Motocross Mike

Mike ducked as a big hand shot through the van window as Bill slowly threaded his way through the crowded parking area. He looked up to see the hand's owner and grabbed it when he saw the smiling face of his racing buddy, Tony Barone. Bill stopped the van as Mike jumped out. The two had not seen each other during the winter months and jostled and joked with one another.

Tony and Mike always pitted together. Tony was from Binghamton about eighty miles from Mike's home but the two young men had always been good friends since their days of racing minibikes. Though seventeen years old, they classified each other as old-timers. They had moved up through the ranks together from minis to the 100cc. Schoolboy class, Amateur and Expert 125cc class and finally, two years ago, 250cc Expert. Upon reaching Expert class, they could apply for a Pro License and run any professional event in the country. Or at least run in the qualifying events for that race.

They called each other old-timers because they had seen so many riders come and go.

Mike and Bill also enjoyed the Barone's hospitality when they raced at Broome-Tioga, the track near Binghamton. Tony and his family always expected them on the Saturday night before the race. Tony's mother would make a huge platter of spaghetti and other Italian delicacies that everyone would enjoy before a good night's sleep in the spacious Barone home.

Charles Loomis

Bill enjoyed these trips because it gave him time to compare notes with Tony's father Mario, who also owned a cycle shop. The two men were always amused at the light-hearted rivalry that the boys carried on at the races, but never allowed it to affect their friendship.

Now, Mario found the van and poked his head in the window and said hello to Bill.

"Hey Bill," he said cheerfully. "Mike looks a little on the skinny side. What's the matter Mike, not enough spaghetti up north? You're not going to beat Tony this year unless you load up on some good stuff down at our house."

Mike laughed, then looked at Tony, with narrowed eyes. "This kid is going to need more than spaghetti power to pass me and my new scoot this year."

"We'll see, we'll see," Tony cut in. "Hang a left over there and go right down to the fence, you'll see our van there. We've got a perfect view of the first turn and the start-finish line. We saved a spot for you."

Mario came around the van. "You guys go on, all your fans are waiting for you. Bill and I will park the van and unload. You got an hour before practice starts. Be ready."

Mike and Tony waved and set out to find friends that they hadn't seen all winter. The first race in the spring was always a

Motocross Mike

reunion of sorts. It was a time to renew old friendships and look over the new bikes of the other competitors.

There were only about ten or twelve riders that Mike and Tony were really interested in. They were the guys who could keep up with them for the first part of any race. Together, they made up the lead pack. Sometimes one of them beat Mike or Tony in the start or over the rough parts of the track because they picked the right line.

But they all knew that Mike and Tony were the kings of the hill. They knew that it wouldn't be a really great race if Mike and Tony weren't able to be there for some reason.

There was much kidding, handshaking and high fives as Mike and Tony made the rounds. The riders all discussed their new bikes or the modifications they had made to their old bikes. Most riders were proud of the modifications done to their bikes. They liked to show them off. If a change proved fast or helped the handling, they were willing to share their ideas with the others.

But there was a lot of tension too. No one would really know who had worked out the hardest or practiced more or who had the fastest bike until the green flag dropped.

After awhile, Mike and Tony broke away from the pack and made their way back to the vans to get into their gear. Another group of friends had gathered there, checking out their shiny, new bikes.

Charles Loomis

"Hey Mike, check out that blonde over on the right, she looks real interested in your bike!"

"Not bad, not bad," Mike replied. But his main attention was drawn to the back of one retreating rider. He was wearing a motocross jersey. It said Ackley on the back in bold letters.

"Hey Tony, " he said under his breath. "Seems I had a visitor, but he didn't even stop to say hello."

Tony followed Mike's gaze. "Don't worry about Ackley, " he said. " By the time this day is over he'll have so much dust in his mouth he won't be able to say hello."

"I'm not worried about him, I would just like to know what's bugging him. You've probably heard that he's after my butt."

"Mike, he isn't going to be anywhere near you when the checkered flag drops."

"We'll see, we'll see," Mike said as he climbed into the back of the van to change into his riding gear.

Mike removed his running shoes, jeans and shirt and folded them carefully on a shelf in the van. He then pulled on his motocross pants and adjusted the hip pads and built-in kneepads. He paused for a minute and ran his hands down his thighs and over his arms thinking, "Okay, guys don't fail me now". There was a spring chill in the air and he decided to wear a sweatshirt under his racing jersey. He buckled his padded leather boots on over

Motocross Mike

two pairs of high socks and slid into his combination shoulder pad/chest protector. He stepped out of the van.

The chest protector protected the rider from rocks flying from the rear tires of the bikes ahead. The shoulder pads helped cushion the impact of a spill. The protector also displayed his name and a big number one on the back to match the number one on the plates on his bike. In the background, he could hear the minis warming up for practice. It was already nine o'clock, but he knew it would be a while before the 250's were allowed on the track for their ten-minute practice session. Just time enough to go over the bike with Bill one more time and get some stretching exercises in. Mike knew how important it was to be "loose" on the bike. Stretching helped avoid injuries.

At last it was time for the 250cc practice. Mike pushed the bike up to the gate that marked the entrance to the track. He kicked the bike over and it came to life with a reassuring roar. Mike blipped the throttle to bring the rpm's up and then backed it off as he threw his leg over. Successive twists of the throttle kept the engine note rising and falling. The sound of sixty other riders doing the same thing seemed to shatter the air. The excitement level soared.

The track attendant waved them on in groups of 4 or 5 as the last of the 125cc's pulled off. Mike watched the riders nearest the gate crowding each other, trying to be polite. But it was impossible to hide their excitement.

Charles Loomis

When it came his turn, Mike made his way around the track carefully and slowly studying the lines in each section. Some overly anxious riders charged the hills and turns as fast as they could, but not Mike. He wanted to memorize the layout before the race began. He wanted to see if any changes had been made from the year before.

After his first lap around the track, he picked up his pace, now passing riders who had whizzed by him during his inspection. He pushed just hard enough to work up a light sweat and finally pulled off the track.

All of a sudden, a rider roared by him-- faster than was allowed at the pit entrance. Mike looked up to see Ackley looking savagely back at him.

"This guy is a real intimidator," he thought as Ackley twisted around and gave him another evil look. A little uneasily, Mike made his way to Bill's van.

He and Bill cleaned the bike up, checked it one more time and waited patiently for the first 250cc moto.

CHAPTER TEN

Mike was on the line. He leaned forward and moved his weight over the gas tank. He stretched his legs behind him, toes touching the ground. He revved the engine higher and higher in anticipation of the start. The board flipped in the starter's hands to reveal the number "one". His eyes shifted from the starter to the first turn and back again concentrating on both.

He slipped the clutch a tiny bit and felt it start to bite. The bike jumped forward a little and he had to haul the clutch all the way in quickly to prevent the front wheel from touching the gate. If the wheel was touching the gate, his section would not drop, leaving him stranded while the other riders roared away. Just as he pulled the clutch all the way in, the starter turned the board sideways and the operator dropped the gate. He swore as he finally got moving-- about midway in the howling mob.

Now, he'd have to waste valuable time passing riders he would ordinarily beat at the start. To his left, a couple of riders were already down, but he concentrated on those ahead of him. The bikes that were on the start line were now funneling down to the first turn, jamming up. So he looked to his left, saw an opening and dove to the outside. He had a clear shot onto the track with only four or five riders ahead of him. He gassed it and moved on the seat to gain maximum traction.

The front wheel came up and skimmed over the ground as he charged for the first turn and the next man ahead of him. He passed him on the first series of whoopdiedoos, shot into another turn and gassed out of it sending up a tall plume of damp earth. He could feel his excitement building. He was less than two bike lengths from third place.

Up ahead was Jim Turner, a good rider that Mike knew and respected from the year before. He would have to pick a good spot to pass him. Jim knew all the tricks that made it hard for another rider to get by. He played fair, but he was tough.

Mike moved within inches of Turner's spinning back wheel. Pressure caused riders to make mistakes and a mistake is a chance to pass. Just ahead of Turner, Mike saw Tony in the lead with Ackley close behind. Ackley was crowding Tony in the turns. Several times, it looked as if he could get by, but he constantly went low and to the inside of every turn-- trying to force Tony up over the berms and off the course. Mike concentrated on Turner and kept up the pressure, waiting for him to make a mistake.

Then, Mike saw his chance. Turner went too fast into a soft berm and slid over it sending dirt and mud flying in all directions. Mike dove to the inside and passed him. The crowd yelled its approval as he roared past the main spectator area.

Now, it was Ackley and Tony. Mike watched closely as they went into a turn, side by side, Ackley sliding up to try to pitch Tony over the top. Mike saw that Ackley was deliberately trying to cause Tony to crash. He was sure of it. But there was nothing he could do. They were riding so recklessly that Mike knew if he got involved all three of them would go down.

From his position, Mike could tell that Tony knew what Ackley was up to. He was pleased to see that Tony was hanging in there, out-maneuvering Ackley on every turn. Mike's only hope was that the officials would realize what was going on and black flag or penalize Ackley. This was unlikely, though because Ackley was careful to make it look good whenever they got near the start-finish area..

Most of the fans didn't know what was going on either, except for people like Bill and Tony's father. The fans were screaming at what they thought was a good race. But but Bill and Mario were swearing under their breath.

Charles Loomis

"I can't believe he's trying to put my kid out of the first race of the season," Mario yelled at Bill.

Meanwhile Mike watched the duel from a safe distance. The two riders in front of him continued to clash. He wanted to get by the battle but could not find an opening. He thought if he did, Ackley might then concentrate on him.

The riders in front of him battled on the brink of disaster through every turn and whoop section. One attacked and the other defended.

Tony was going into the turns lower and lower to give himself room to maneuver against Ackley's attacks. Ackley hardly had any room to get into the turns below Tony. When he did and began to slide up on him, Tony slid up to the berm and powered out again.

But it was obvious, that Ackley was the more powerful rider. It was only a matter of time before his strategy was successful.

The race was now at the halfway point. Mike continued to dodge mud and rocks thrown up from the rear wheels of the two dueling riders in front of him. He watched as the two began to tire from the battle. Mike could rest a bit and pick the best lines around the track. No other rider had challenged him since he passed Turner. But now the slower riders in the back of the pack were coming into view as the three front runners prepared to lap them.

Motocross Mike

Then it happened. Tony went into a turn a little too fast. He locked up both front and rear brakes and momentarily lost control. Just then Ackley slid in from the side and pushed him over the berm. Tony went down heavily on his shoulder as his bike flipped off to the side of the track. He did not move.

Mike saw it all in slow motion. Stunned to see his friend go down so hard. He looked over his shoulder at Tony lying motionless on the ground as he went by. He felt a surge of anger and his first reaction was to go after Ackley. But thoughts of his friend lying hurt by the track overtook him. He slowed, turned off the track and raced back to Tony. There would be other races. Other chances to make up lost points.

A flagman and a couple of spectators were kneeling over Tony.

Mike leaned his bike up against the fence and ran over.

"Don't move him," he shouted. He removed his gloves, goggles and helmet and bent over Tony.

"Tony, you okay?" he said as he knelt beside his friend.

Tony only moaned. Mike assumed he must have been knocked unconscious for a short period. The flagman signaled for the ambulance crew and they came running across the field. Mike moved everyone back away from Tony as he lay there moaning. Mike heard him say something about pain in his leg.

Charles Loomis

He knelt down and put his hand on his friend's arm as Tony rocked painfully back and forth in the grass by the track.

"My leg, my leg," Tony groaned. "I think it's broken."

Mike carefully loosened some of Tony's riding gear as the ambulance crew arrived.

"You'll be okay, Buddy," Mike said as he stepped aside to let the medical technicians work on Tony.

Tony looked up at Mike with eyes full of anger. "Mike the race is still on. Get out there and whip that bastard."

"I'm on my way. You take care now."

Mike ran to his bike. He had lost a lap and knew he couldn't win but he wanted to race next to Ackley for a lap or two. As he started his bike, he saw Bill and Mario running to Tony. He rocketed out onto the track--sending a shower of dirt and mud onto nearby spectators.

The race was almost over. The white flag signaling one more lap had already been flashed to the leaders. He came out on the track right behind the leaders. He realized that Ackley must be just ahead of him. A flood of rage came over him. He gassed it and rode faster than he ever had in practice. The crowd watched in awe as he flew off the jumps and bumps and climbed hills as if they weren't even there. In his fury Mike raced to catch the rider that had intentionally hurt his friend.

Motocross Mike

He overtook some of the leaders so fast, they didn't even see him coming. Then Ackley was just yards ahead. He didn't know what he was going to do when he caught him, but he knew he had to cross the finish line ahead of him. He knew he couldn't win because of the lost lap but he was determined to pass Ackley. No matter what.

Ackley didn't know that Mike was back in the race. He was just cruising to the checkered flag, sure now, of his victory.

Mike blasted up behind him and put his front wheel just inches behind Ackley's back wheel. Thoughts rushed through Mike's mind. " I want Ackley to know I'm here. I want him to know what real pressure is. "

"Come on big boy, make a mistake," Mike said into his helmet.

Ackley sensed his presence. His eyes registered surprise as he glanced over his shoulder to find Mike right behind him. Mike kept bearing down, practically pushing him through the corners. He could feel the pain, anger and frustration welling up in his chest. For one of the few times in his life he was experiencing hatred - hatred for this mean, crazy person who had hurt his friend.

Ackley picked up the pace and went as fast as he dared. As much as he wanted to show up Mike, he wanted to win the moto

Charles Loomis

even more. The faster he went, the harder Mike pushed, showing Ackley his front wheel whenever he could.

The crowd was again on their feet, cheering. Mike wasn't even aware of them. He only saw Ackley's back and could feel only rage as he swooped through the turns and over the big whoops, pushing Ackley to his limit.

Mike found a chance to pass just before the finish line. Ackley went into a turn tight, hoping to cut Mike off. Mike kept the power on and slid sideways, hitting the big, soft berm on the outside of the turn. He threw so much mud and dirt into the air that the crowd gasped. They thought he had gone down.

But Mike was just fine. In a demonstration of perfect control, he shifted down and powered out of the turn just ahead of Ackley. It was a smooth maneuver and it had caught Ackley completely off guard.

Mike crossed the finish line first. But Ackley had won the race. Ackley took the checkered flag and made his way to the pit area.

The crowd hardly noticed. They were cheering Mike. Word of Ackley's ride had spread like wildfire when Tony went down. Mike pulled off the track as quickly as he could and rode through the pit area to where they were loading Tony into the ambulance. He gently pushed Mario aside in his haste to see his friend before he left for the hospital.

"Tony, how's it going?"

"They think my leg is broken and a possible concussion. It's a good thing we wear brain buckets."

"Why that dirty-----," Mike began.

Tony raised his hand. "Hey man, don't get mad, just beat the pants off that guy in the next moto, will ya? Just for me."

"I'll do it for both of us. That guy has got it coming."

"You'll have to let us go now," the ambulance driver said as he motioned Mike away from the ambulance.

Mike waved to Tony. He and Bill and Mario turned to help load the Barone's van for the trip to the hospital.

"Did you see what that idiot was doing to Tony?" Mike asked.

"Yeah, I saw okay," Mario nodded. "I saw real good."

Mario suddenly turned and started toward Ackley's van. Mike and Bill knew what he had on his mind. They grabbed Mario and pushed him back in the direction of their own vans. Mario pushed back in his efforts to get to Ackley.

"No, Mario," Bill commanded. "This is the boys fight. They're big boys now, let them take care of it in their own way. You need to go to the hospital to be with Tony."

"Mario, believe me," Mike said. "I feel the same way. I want to go over there and show him a few wrestling holds that aren't in the book. But the best way to put this guy away is right on the track. Even Tony said that. I'm going to do it and so is Tony as soon as his leg is healed up."

"Mike, his leg is broken, he's gonna be lucky if he rides at all this season," Mario moaned and put his hands to his face in despair. "Okay, do it your way. You're right, Ackley wants that number one plate and he'll do anything to get it. We'll just make sure he doesn't get it. Anything you need, Mike – anything – you just let old Mario know and you got it, kid. If your old pal Bill ain't got it, you just give me a call and I'll have it for you if I have to fly clear to California to get it. You beat this creep, you hear me Mike?."

"I hear you, Mario. And thanks.." Mike said as he patted the heartsick father on the back.

A friend of Mike's had been pushing his bike along behind them. Mike thanked him and took the bike from him as they made their way back to the van. A small crowd waited near Bill's van.

A fan came forward and shook Mike's hand. "That was a beautiful move you put on Ackley in that last turn, Mike. You should have seen the dirt fly when you hit that berm. Everybody thought you went down. I'll bet Ackley was surprised. We all know what he did to Tony. You can beat him and we all want to see it."

Motocross Mike

"Thanks," Mike nodded as he stripped off his wet and muddy gear. "I'm going to be doing my best out there. Now, I've got more reason than ever."

Mike busied himself cleaning his bike as he waited for the second 250cc moto. Bill checked every nut and bolt he could get a wrench on. The bike had been well prepared, so there was very little to do. Mike went over to the fence and watched the 100cc class race. The little engines whined to a high pitch. Mike watched the leaders go by. He wondered which of them would be the "champs" of tomorrow.

CHAPTER ELEVEN

Standing by the fence, Mike was approached by a number of his fans. Everyone, it seemed wanted to ask him about his injuries from the previous year, and one or two of them offered their comments about Ackley's ride. But Mike was not in the mood for small talk. He wanted to be by himself. He needed to plan for the next race. So he retreated to the van and crawled inside. He was angry, about what had happened to Tony, but at the same time, he knew that anger wouldn't help. He needed to keep his cool . What he really needed was to beat Ackley fair and square. That meant he'd have to stay out of trouble and just out ride him.

Bill left Mike to himself. He knew Mike needed time to think, to sort things out and consider race strategy. Figuring out a guy like Ackley was going to be tough, and Bill knew it. Mike's mom had brought him up in an atmosphere of love and caring for other

Motocross Mike

people. And Bill knew from experience that Mike found it hard to understand meanness in himself or anybody else.

The other races came off without incident-- three classes of 100cc, and three of 125cc. Finally, the 250 expert class was called to the start area. Mike pulled his gear back on. The spring air had turned colder and he slipped a jacket over his shoulders as he and Bill made their way to the start line. The 250 amateurs were heading off the track as they got there. Mike listened as the starter called the expert class riders to the line in order of their finish in the first moto. He called Ackley first because he had finished first. Because he'd lost a lap in the previous race, Mike was one of the last ones to be called. He selected a place on the line near the end. He chose the end spot because it looked like he'd get good traction. Because of the end spot, he had farther to go, so he would need all the traction he could get.

Ackley watched him carefully from his line at the inside. As Mike glanced up, their eyes locked, just long enough for Mike to see the cold determination there..

Mike was still a little puzzled by it all. It was hard to understand a rider like Ackley. If he was so good, why had he needed to hurt Tony that way? Why couldn't he have just won it fair and square?

Still, Mike felt more determined than ever to win this race. Winning was more important than ever.

Charles Loomis

As the last of the 250 amateurs left the track, the riders on the line started their engines and revved them. All around them, excitement and tension filled the air. Mike kept thinking about Ackley. About how good it was going to feel when he beat him. His anger made him almost nervous--an unfamiliar feeling this close to the start.

Bill stood behind him. He noticed Mike's uneasiness, but dismissed it as the jitters. He reached out and gave Mike's shoulder a reassuring squeeze as he took his jacket. Mike never took his eyes off the starter. He knew when the board went sideways, the gate would drop very quickly.

He shifted his weight forward and double checked to make sure his bike was in second gear. He made sure the gas was on. Over the years, he'd seen many riders have perfect starts only to find themselves stalled out at the first turn because they had forgotten to turn on the gas. Mike always used second gear for starts. It gave him just the right combination of speed and power. He rolled the throttle on and off. The bikes on the line screamed as the riders anticipated the start. Mike's eyes were glued to the gate. He would take off at the first sign of its movement.

The starter glanced at his watch and turned the big number one board to the riders. The flagman hovered nearby and watched the gate intently. When the board turned sideways, it switched the start of the race to the gate operator. He could drop the gate anytime in the next fifteen seconds but most operators dropped it quickly after the board reached the sideways position.

The gate dropped. They were off. Mike popped the clutch a little too quickly. The bike got immediate traction and slid him back on the seat just enough to let the front wheel come up too high. He struggled momentarily with his balance and control and almost lost it in a loop over backwards. He uttered an oath. "I practiced this a million times", he thought furiously.

He got control again and jumped on the gas. He made up a lot of ground quickly. He aimed at the wooden post marking the first turn and ran straight for it, hoping to make his turn onto the track right at that point. Two other riders had the same idea. They were slower than Mike and hadn't noticed his problems on the start line. It never occurred to them to worry about riders coming up from behind at nearly twice their speed. They cut for the same spot that Mike had picked out. He couldn't stop. They had him boxed in. All three of them came together in a terrible tangle.

Mike felt a twinge of pain in his right hand and pulled it away from the handle bar as he went down in the mess. Bodies and bikes flailed around as each rider tried to untangle himself and his bike from the accident.

Mike got free first and jumped on his bike. He reached for the throttle and with a sinking heart realized that it wasn't where it should be. He looked and now understood why he had felt the pain in his hand. The bar was bent down at an extreme angle. He twisted the throttle and to his amazement it still worked. His mind worked at lightning speed as he made his decision. Unless something else was wrong, he would try to run the race. He kicked the bike back to life, glanced back and took off, leaving the other two riders still flailing in the mud.

He was way back in the pack. The bike was almost impossible to ride and balance. The handlebars were just too damaged to hang onto, but there was no time to change them. But he was determined to finish the race. Over the jumps the bike was unpredictable and the huge bumps in the whoopdiedoo sections almost threw him off. He hung on doggedly.

The fans were dejected. They'd expected Ackley to "get his" from Mike this time out. They jeered and booed as Ackley made his way triumphantly around the track.

Jim Turner challenged him from time to time, but he was no match for the strong and talented Ackley. He was obviously enjoying himself, "styling" for the crowd, launching high off the jumps and pulling wheelies in front of the biggest groups of spectators. He didn't care if they booed him or not. In Ackley's mind, today was the day he would show Mike Porter that he was no longer king of the hill.

He was lapping Mike now, and roosted him at a particularly muddy section as he sped by

Motocross Mike

Mike passed Bill five times and Bill frantically tried to wave him off the track. He and the bike were black with mud. Stooped over in the unnatural riding position because of the bent handlebars, Mike was the picture of defeat. But, he would finish. And finish he did-- to the whoops and cheers of all his friends and fans.

Mike was the hero at Royal Mountain that day--not Ackley. Not one person congratulated him. Furious, he threw his bike in his van and drove out of the track at a breakneck speed.

"Mail my check to me," he yelled belligerently to the track owner as he roared past the office.

The reactions of Mike's supporters buoyed his spirits. The feelings of humiliation at his defeat, his loss of concentration and just foolish riding soon left him. He was especially happy to hear that Tony's break was without complications and that he would be out of his cast in four or five weeks. Time enough to finish up the season.

"Hey Mike," one of his pals called out. "There's always next week. You'll get him."

Mike managed a small laugh. "Seems like we've been saying that a lot around here lately. Right, Bill?"

"I guess so," Bill smiled.

CHAPTER TWELVE

That night, Mike and Bill arrived home at about seven and unloaded the van in silence. It had not been a particularly successful day. Mike's hand had been badly bruised when his handlebars were bent. He'd kept it wrapped in ice from the cooler all the way home.

Once inside Bill's house, they went to raid the refrigerator and call Mike's mother. Bill's wife, Janice Maslak was watching television and asked how they had done. While Mike was on the phone, Bill reported on their dismal day. He could hear the beginnings of an argument developing over the phone.

"Mom," Mike protested. "It could have happened to anybody. I just made a small mistake and had to pay for it, that's all." There was a pause. "Okay, I'll be right home."

"She's not coming over for coffee, Mike?"

Janice called out.

Motocross Mike

"No," Mike said a little sullenly. "She'll probably never come over again. At least not if Bill's here."

"Now, what did I do?" Bill protested.

"You took me racing, I guess. I had to tell her about my hand and naturally she started in."

"What are we going to do with her?" Bill asked shaking his head. "Come on, I'll take you home."

They took the short route to Mike's house. It was a cool spring evening.

Bill tried to smooth things over. "Like I said Mike, let's not be too tough on her. She went through a lot with your Dad's accident."

"I know, I know, but I get so tired of it. I understand where she's coming from, I really do. But every time I cough it's because of motocross. I'd like to think it's going to get better but the closer I get to graduation the worse it gets. She just pushes the college thing without any thought of what I want to do. I want to go into engineering, something to do with motorcycles. I want that just as much as she does, but not before I get racing out of my system. Does she think I'd be doing anything any different if Dad were alive?"

"Well, we'll just have to keep working on her little by little."

"That's easy for you to say, you're going home."

Bill laughed. "Yeah, I guess so. See you after school tomorrow, kid. Good luck."

Mike stepped down from the van and slung his equipment bag over his shoulder. "Good night Bill and thanks for everything. It really means a lot to have your help."

Bill shot an uncomfortable look in Mike's direction. "Hey, no problem. You know I'm having a good time too. See you."

He backed the van out of the driveway as Mike made his way to the house. "Here we go," Mike thought darkly. He felt like he was being cast into a lion's den.

"Hi, Mom. I'm home," he said in his most cheerful voice.

"Hello," she replied coolly. "Let me see your hand."

"Ahh--Mom, it's nothing, really."

She looked at it carefully and suddenly burst into tears. "Michael," she said between sobs. "I have worked and slaved and deprived myself to save money for your college education. I have nursed you though sickness, given you practically everything a child growing up could want, and you do this to me."

"Mom, please. I appreciate everything you've done for me. Believe me I didn't do this to hurt you, but I have to live my life a little bit for me, too."

Ann Porter wiped away at her tears. "I can't stand to see you hurt!" she said.

Motocross Mike

Mike sighed heavily. "Mom," he went on. "Motocross is part of me. It's what I want most right now. I've told you a hundred times that I do want to go to college. I'm even looking forward to it. I think I'd love engineering or something like that. But I can do that later. Right now, I want to race."

"But suppose you get hurt real bad?"

He held her trembling hand in his. "Mom, I understand. I know how much you loved Dad. Sometimes I think that I like to race so much because I love him too. Because I think that it's something he'd want me to do. But you've got to admit that I'd be racing if he were still alive. I can't understand why you can't see that."

"If he were alive it would be different. I can't bear the thought of losing another person I love to motorcycle racing."

"Mom, come on. Motocross is not a terribly dangerous sport if you stay in shape. Bill Harris got the worse injury of his career on a jet ski. George Moore was killed riding his bicycle. Do you think I would do anything that I thought would get myself killed? I wouldn't do that to myself and I certainly wouldn't do it to you. If you'd only just lighten up a bit and not worry so much."

"Not worry, not worry!" she exclaimed. "You come home with broken ribs, cracked collar bones, bumps and bruises and you tell me not to worry?"

Charles Loomis

"Mom, those injuries last fall were the worst I've had in six years. When you get right down to it, they weren't really that bad."

"Not bad? They were bad enough to keep you out of school for three weeks."

"Mom, come on. You know why I stayed out of school. It wasn't the injuries."

Mike decided to stop talking. They weren't accomplishing anything.

Ann noticed his silence. "You are your father's son. As soon as we start talking about the real problems, you stop talking."

"Mom, I'm tired and hungry. And we've been over all this before."

She sighed. "You're right. Let's get some ice for your hand. But Michael, we've got to solve this somehow. This is not the end of it."

"I know, Mom, I know."

CHAPTER THIRTEEN

He saw Chub in school the next day, and gave him the low down on the weekend's races.

"I told you Ackley was going to be real trouble. I found out all about him at an enduro I ran down in New Jersey. A friend of mine from the district where he used to live said Ackley told him he was moving up here and one of his main goals was to kick your butt."

"The guy's trouble all right," Mike agreed. "But I can handle that. The main problem is – he's mean. That makes him unpredictable. I want to go pro this year, Chub. I'd hate to have what he did to Tony happen to me. That would really mess up my plans. Last year was bad enough."

"Just keep at least an inch ahead of him. And he'll be no problem. Besides, you're good enough to give him some of his own medicine. Even if you do it just for old Tony's sake. Nobody's going to hold it against you."

"I know, but I don't want to ride that way, and I don't want to win that way, either. It's just not right. "

"He ought to be barred from racing at all, " Chub put in,

"Definitely, " Mike agreed. "But deep down, I think the worst thing that could happen to Ackley is to get beaten fair and square. No matter what stuff he tries to pull. I think that would get to him more than anything. So I'm just going to run him until his tongue is dragging on the track!"

Chub grinned. "I'd like to see that."

Mike returned his smile. "Come along with us next week, you can watch me in action."

"Aw, heck, " Chub replied frowning. "We're planting corn. I don't think I can go." All at once he brightened. "Unless it rains."

When Mike went to work that afternoon the shop was busy.. It had been a beautiful, warm spring day and cycle enthusiasts poured in to examine and order the new models. Mike and the other mechanics were up to their ears with work.

It was so hectic, Mike didn't have a chance to look at his race bike until after the shop closed. He was a little anxious. He was afraid it might have sustained more damage than he was aware of. He went to work cleaning it up from the previous day's mud bath

Motocross Mike

and changed the bent handlebars. He promised himself he'd take it out for a practice run the following day after school. Because of the bent bars he had to ride it so slow after the crash he couldn't be sure that it was okay until he'd gotten it fully up to speed..

After locking up, Bill returned to the shop area.

"How's that hand of yours coming along?" he asked.

"Okay, I guess." Mike answered. He flexed it for Bill's benefit. The swelling had gone down and the bruises looked fainter than they had before.

Bill nodded approvingly. "That'll be fine by the weekend, " he said. "You shouldn't have any trouble with it." He paused and met Mike's eyes. "So, have you figured out how you're going to beat this Ackley guy?"

"I think so, " Mike replied.." I ran with him long enough yesterday to get an idea of how he rides. He's strong, but I think I can wear him down over the long haul."

"Providing he doesn't put you in the same hospital with Tony." Bill answered grimly.

"We'll see. I think I'll start running again in the mornings, though."

Bill raised his eyebrows. "Looks like you really mean business, young fella."

Mike looked intently at Bill. "I hate to see any rider get racked up that way. But when it's Tony, it really gets me hot."

Charles Loomis

"Don't let it throw you, kid." Bill said. "Use your anger. Ride it. But don't let it distract you. Nobody wins that way. Now," he went on. "Get out of here will you? Go home and see your mom for a change."

The next morning Mike slowly roused from a deep sleep. He could hear music coming from somewhere far away and some crazed person saying how great it was to be alive on such a beautiful day, urging all sleepy heads to wake up and get out of bed. With a start, Mike realized it was his clock radio. He wished he had a rock to throw at it. He opened one eye and saw the digits indicating it was six o'clock – time to run.

He looked out the window and could see that it was indeed going to be a beautiful day. Still he longed for the warmth and comfort of his bed. He liked to keep in shape, but sometimes the sacrifices necessary were almost unbearable. It was still nippy outside in the mornings so he slipped his heavy warm-ups on over his running gear, pulled a knit cap and gloves on and headed out the door. His mother was still sleeping and he closed the door quietly. He did some stretching exercises, then worked up to a brisk pace as he headed down the road towards the shop. On the way back he would stop at Bill and Janice's for a quick cup of coffee.

Mike went two miles past the shop, down the hill and over the course he had measured out. At the bottom of the hill, he turned, already knowing how he would really feel the uphill run in his whole body. He strained and sprinted the last one hundred yards to Bill's house. Bill and Janice watched him cross the frosty grass to their front door from the picture window in their family room.

"You're looking at a strong kid, Janice. Look at him go those last few yards. He's in better shape now than I ever was. He's going to make pro this year."

"Bill, do me a favor, " Janice replied. "Please don't talk like that in front of Ann. She's sick from worry."

"I know, but one of these days I've got to sit down and seriously speak to her about Mike."

"Don't you think that's up to Mike? You do an awful lot for him. Maybe this is one battle he should fight alone."

"What do you mean I do a lot for him? I don't do any more than any other sponsor does for his rider."

"Oh, come on Bill. He's like a son to you and you know it."

"So what? I'm still not going to spoil him." Bill grumped as he went to open the door for Mike.

Mike stood on the doorstep catching his breath. "Whew, right now I'm feeling real bad that I quit running over the winter. I'm dying."

Bill laughed. "Cup of coffee, kid?"

"Yeah, and a nice big glass of water."

"Coming right up," Janice called cheerfully from the kitchen.

Charles Loomis

Mike downed the water and settled into one of the Maslak's comfortable kitchen chairs.

"Breakfast, Hon?" Janice asked as she always did.

"No thanks Janice, I'll eat with Mom."

"Well, Mike, " Bill asked. "Ready to take on Ackley at Broome-Tioga this Sunday?"

"I think so. These poor starts I've been getting can't last forever. I'm going to practice starts some more this week."

"Take some extra time if you need it. We can handle the shop without you

for another hour each day."

"Maybe I'll take you up on that and put in a real long, hard session on Thursday."

Janice was smiling. She sneaked a peak at Bill and mouthed at him, "I don't spoil him."

Bill ignored her and turned again to Mike. "Okay, we'll see to it."

Mike finished his coffee and headed for the door. "Thanks, Janice. See you folks later."

Mike trotted to his house and found his mother preparing breakfast. "Good morning, Mike, you're up kind of early aren't you?"

"Morning Mom. I decided to start running again."

"Oh, I thought you felt you were in good enough shape."

Motocross Mike

"Every little bit helps." He kissed his mother on the cheek.

Mike and Bill had not told Ann Porter about the developing rivalry with Walter Ackley. As he watched her preparing eggs and toast, Mike was glad he hadn't mentioned it. About the last thing he needed right now was more trouble. That afternoon Mike suited up and ran his bike on the practice track. To his relief, it was fine. He went back to the shop, picked up his practice bike and gave himself a good, hard thirty-minute workout. Sweating and breathing heavily he rode down to his house, took off his practice clothes, showered, and rode his bike over the short trail back to the shop. He was happy. He had never felt better physically in his life. I'm ready for anything Ackley has to dish out, he thought.

Tuesday, Wednesday and Thursday he repeated the routine. Friday was a rest day, and Saturdays at the shop were always busy. The weather for the whole week had been unusually warm and motorcycle enthusiasts had turned out in droves. Normally they closed at noon on Saturday but it was two o'clock before Bill could push the last customers out the door and lock it behind them.

"Whew!" he said to his head mechanic Jim Mazzoli, "What a day! Man, these guys want the new bikes bad."

"I guess so. I could have sold ten "Super Streaks" if we had them in stock." Jim replied.

Charles Loomis

Oh well, we've got to make it while we can, winter's are long and cold. I'll cash up and check everything out. Why don't you go on home and enjoy the rest of the day."

"Thanks Bill, I'll see you Monday. Good luck tomorrow, Mike"

"Thanks, Jim." Mike said with a wave. "Have a great weekend."

Bill cashed up, gave the shop a once over, straightened out some merchandise and joined Mike in the back.

"All set for tomorrow, kid?"

"I think so, no major problems. Everything's working fine."

"I'm going back to the house for a sandwich. Want one?"

"Sure," Mike answered barely looking up from his bike. "Sounds good."

Over in his kitchen, Bill chuckled.

"What so funny?" his wife, Janine asked.

"I just asked Mike how the bike was and he said "fine". If I know him, he'll have that thing taken apart and put back together again before the afternoon is out. He's not leaving anything to chance tomorrow."

"You haven't told Ann about this Ackley guy yet, have you?"

"No."

"Don't you think you should? She's bound to hear how Tony broke his leg sooner or later."

"Maybe. But you said I should let Mike handle it. He didn't want to tell her so I said okay."

"I'm sorry dear, I did say that. There's sandwiches in the frig for you and Mike."

Bill carried the sandwiches back to the shop. He and Mike chatted as they worked. Mike concentrated on race prep for the bike and Bill loaded the van for the next day's race. They finished about five o'clock.

"Come on over about five in the morning. I'll rustle us up some breakfast and we'll be on our way to Broome-Tioga."

Five thirty the next morning they were on the road. "I wonder if Tony and Mario will be there?" Bill asked.

"I think so. They would love to see me fix that guy's wagon."

"Mike, I know I don't have to tell you this again, but just race your own race. Don't let that clown sucker you into anything where he gets a chance to hurt you. Stay on the inside whenever you can. If he pulls some of the stuff that he pulled on Tony, just lay back and wait for an opening. And don't dice with him. If you don't nail this guy today, we'll get him eventually. I know that for sure. Just don't get hurt, okay? We've got a lot of business to take care of this year."

Charles Loomis

"Yeah, I know, Bill. If I can just get around my mother," he said as he reclined his seat to get some rest on the way to the track.

CHAPTER FOURTEEN

The crowd at Broome-Tioga was enthusiastic. This track had been the scene of many national races over the years and the spectators knew their stuff when it came to motocross. They loved the local races there almost as much as the Nationals.

Mike and Bill went through the usual race preparations. Mike easily qualified for the two motos in the main events.

Finally, it was time.

The 250's lined up for the first moto. Mike and Ackley had both drawn low numbers. Ackley waited for Mike to pick his spot and then moved right in next to him with a sneer. Mike ignored him. Bill stood between the two riders.

"Intimidation works both ways," he said to Mike. Mike caught a glimpse of Mario and Tony in the sidelines. Mario waved and Tony waggled his cast in the air as high as he could get it. Mike grinned and gave them a "thumbs up". He then turned his attention to the starter.

The board started to turn. He felt Bill's hand patting him on the back. All around him, the noise increased to an ear shattering pitch as the riders anticipated the start. The board went sideways and the gate dropped. He was on his way. He'd had a good start at last and he knew it.

He concentrated on the turn on to the track. He knew Ackley was close. He could almost feel his presence. As he made the turn, he caught sight of Ackley's black boots and yellow pants. He was right on his back.

"Let's give him a couple of fast laps and see how he holds up," Mike thought. Mike watched the track carefully for any change in lines, new rocks surfacing or bumps. He cranked it on and the crowd went wild as he literally soared and left Ackley ten, then twenty, then fifty yards behind.

The faces along the fence became a blur and the cheers a faint echo in his helmet as he swooped gracefully through turns, power sliding like he was on a flat tracker. He threw up sprays of loose earth on every turn. He was moving fast!

Mike's speed caught Ackley completely off guard. He blipped his throttle on over a jump and landed too heavy on the back wheel. He almost looped the bike over backward. His legs splayed out as he fought for balance. The crowd hooted and booed thinking that he was beaten. But Ackley wasn't beaten yet--just surprised. He bore down on Mike like a lion after a gazelle. He was a good rider and he knew it. Above all, he didn't like to lose.

Ackley settled down and rode his hardest. He wasn't as smooth as Mike but could out-muscle the bike where Mike outrode him. He picked up the pace dramatically, slamming into corners and literally flying off the jumps. His bike was screaming as he pushed it to higher and higher revs. He began to close the gap between him and Mike in each successive lap. Never had he ridden against a rider who pushed it to the limit from the first.

"Next moto, Porter " he vowed to himself. "I'll show you what it means to push."

The crowd, was out of control. Mike could see the yelling faces and outstretched fists twisting in the air in an imitation of turning the throttle. On each sharp turn he could see Ackley, not gaining much, but staying right with him.

Mike grudgingly admitted to Ackley's skill. The guy was tough. Mike kept it dialed on. Being in the lead had distinct advantages. He could pick his own lines and maneuver about the track unhampered by riders to the left or the right of him. This advantage lasted, of course, until he started lapping the field.

Lapped riders could be passed rather easily if they held their lines. But usually they were the poorer or newer riders, unsure of their skills. They might bobble and move into an overtaking rider's line by mistake. Sometimes the less experienced tried to test themselves by trying to stay with a leader. In either case, it could be dangerous. A smart lapped rider moved out of the way . A dumb one sometimes got in the way.

Every rider in district three knew about the rivalry between Mike and Ackley. Anyone who would get in the way of this freight train on rubber wheels moving up on them would have to be very stupid. This rider dutifully moved towards the side of the track to let Mike and his shadow thunder on by. Together, Mike and Ackley passed three more riders in quick succession. No one challenged them. No one even dared.

Old "number three", as Jim Turner was beginning to call himself, was a hundred yards behind. He was content to battle it out with the three riders challenging his position and was almost happy that he didn't have to contend with Mike and Ackley.

Mike came around to the finish line and got the white flag. One more lap to go. He kept the throttle on. He was determined to win. If he could only hold Ackley off for this lap. On a corner, he glanced over his shoulder and Ackley was right there, ten yards away. He picked up the pace on the next corner and glanced around. Ackley was still right there. He flew off the lip of a steep downhill and defied gravity for sixty or seventy feet. He landed at the bottom of the gully they called "Down and Out" utilizing every inch of suspension. He came down on the seat so hard, he

Motocross Mike

bounced off it just in time to set up for the steep, bumpy uphill side of the gully. He came out of the gully and flew another fifty feet. Looking over his shoulder, he saw Ackley now ten feet away just waiting for him to make a mistake.

He felt good but the enormous amount of concentration was taxing him to his limits. His respect for Ackley as a rider grew. Ackley now "showed him a wheel" on the turns. But Mike hung on. "This is my race and you're not taking it away from me, buddy," he thought.

Meanwhile, Bill, Mario and Tony were going out of their minds. Bill had long ago tossed the chalkboard aside. Mike didn't need the board to know where Ackley was, that much was for sure. He went from board signals to jumping up and down to wringing his hands. Tony had cheered himself hoarse and there were tear streaks on Mario's face.

Later, Mike would say it was the toughest race he had ever been in.

Yet all his efforts paid off as he crossed the line inches ahead of Ackley. He stood up on the pegs and threw his hands up in the air. The cheering crowd went wild as Mike made his way to the pits. He was tired but happy. Bill took his bike as he collapsed into a lawn chair. He pulled off his helmet and his sweaty hair hung in loose strands.

Bill got him some Gatorade and a cool, wet towel. He couldn't conceal his happiness. "What a race!. I don't believe it. You were fantastic." Was all he could say over and over.

Suddenly, both froze as they looked up at Ackley standing in front of them. His face was red with rage and the effort of the race. His hair was a sopping mess. He had twice as much dirt and dust packed on him as Mike because he had been following so closely. He looked like something out of a bad dream. He pointed a finger at Mike.

"You better get plenty of rest turkey. Because next moto – you're mine." He turned briskly and walked away.

Mario and Tony had arrived on the scene about the same time as Ackley. For a moment everybody was speechless. Tony finally broke the silence.

"I don't believe it. That guy is crazy."

Mike nodded. "Crazy, yes. But also fast. I found that out."

"Aw come on, you had him all the way, Mike." Tony protested.

"Tony, I was pushing as hard as I could all the way. He was right there."

Mario came over and offered his hand. "You did real good, kid. Now go out and get him the second moto."

Mike rested while Bill busied himself checking and cleaning the bike for the second moto. The call came for the second 250 moto and Bill pushed the bike over to the start line for Mike. Mike had first choice of starting positions. Ackley had second. Once again, Ackley pushed his bike right in next to Mike's.

"This guy is something else." Bill said quietly to Mike.

Mike adjusted his gear, swung his leg over and started the bike as the 125's pulled off the track. He wondered what kind of surprise Ackley was planning for him this time. The starter positioned the board, the gate dropped and they were off.

This time, they both got a good start. Side by side, they headed for the turn onto the track. Mike had the inside and held it. He was in the lead when they hit the track, with Ackley right on his rear fender. He hit the whoops as fast as he could go. Ackley was skirting disaster. He obviously knew it. Mike could tell he was almost out of control when Ackley passed him. He was going to muscle the bike up the hill. It was one of the more impressive feats of strength and daring that Mike had ever seen.

Ackley's bike was careening from side to side in what motocrossers call a "tank slapper". Rocks and dirt pelted Mike as Ackley went by. The bike continued its wild course up and over the top of the hill.

Smooth is better, Mike thought as he rode the bumps over the top. When he got there, he couldn't believe the distance that Ackley had put on him and he got on the gas-- hard.

Charles Loomis

Ackley rode as if he was being chased by demons. Mike kept him a steady distance in front to see if he could wear him down. He couldn't. He kept the same blistering pace. Half way through the second lap Mike felt he should make his move. Forcing himself to the very limit of control he inched up on Ackley. And then, a strange thing happened. He was right on Ackley's back wheel. It seemed that Ackley had slowed and had deliberately let Mike catch up.

Maybe he's got mechanical problems Mike thought. I can't believe he's going to let me by.

Ackley pulled to the inside of a left turn hairpin and let Mike have the outside. They were on the backside of the track, no officials watching. Mike hit the berm and powered out. Out of the corner of his eye he could see Ackley's front wheel heading right for him.

"The fool is going to T-bone me," Mike thought. Mike swerved to the right and slid sideways into Ackley and bounced off him. It was a good move. Both riders went down but neither was hurt. At the same time both jumped back up and were off before anyone knew what happened.

Mike thought about what Bill had said to him – "Don't let him sucker you into anything. Stay on the inside."

"Well, that's not going to happen again", he vowed. "I'll just wait for the right place to pass."

The right place didn't come. Ackley rode as good as anyone Mike had ever seen. Mike was unnerved by the threat of Ackley's move in the big corner. He couldn't believe that anyone would risk injury to himself or mechanical damage to his own bike in order to take another rider out. It just wasn't done.

Mike stayed behind, waiting for Ackley to make a mistake. He pushed and strained to keep the pressure on, but his rival didn't waiver. He'd picked his lines well and held them right to the finish line. Both riders crossed the line exhausted. Ackley turned in his seat and gave Mike the finger. Mike just shook his head in disbelief as he made his way to the pits. Ackley had won another race. The rules state that in case of a tie the first rider in the second moto, is the winner.

CHAPTER FIFTEEN

Mike was bummed. Bill drove through the valley that led home in the fading daylight. They both had lapsed into silence. There was nothing more to say about the race. His head filled with self-criticism and doubt, Mike leaned his head back against the seat and spoke.

"Bill, maybe I'm not tough enough to go pro."

"What?" Bill shot back. "What are you talking about?"

Mike smacked a fist into his hand in frustration. "Look at Ackley, that guy is tough. He has a lot of nerve and doesn't seem to crack at all under pressure. No matter how hard I push him he doesn't waiver."

Bill punched the air with his forefinger. "You can't seem to do a head trip on him, but it sounds like he's getting to you alright."

"I don't understand him, I just wish I knew."

Motocross Mike

"You can't possibly know what's going on in his head, Mike. Maybe it's all for show. If you're starting to believe it, it's a damn good show. If it isn't a show and he really is that ornery then it's going to catch up to him. He can't concentrate on business if he's got that much hate in him. You keep pressing him like you are and I guarantee you that he'll crack. If he really is that mean and has that much ambition, he's probably not sleeping much at night and he's probably over training which together is going to wear him to a frazzle. You watch and see. Hell, Mike, he moved all the way up to district 3 just to nail you because he knows the factory boys are watching you. He probably figures if he buries you, then they'll have to take him on their team."

"That makes sense. I'm just having a lot of problems handling the whole situation."

"You're handling it fine. Just keep on doing what you're doing and it will all come out perfect."

"What bothered me most today was that I really couldn't get by him in the second moto. I waited for him to make a slip but he hung right in there. I've never had that happen to me before."

"Ah ha, now we're getting to it. Mike, this is the best competition you've ever had. Sure, Tony is good but he's not as good as Ackley. You're just flustered because somebody came along to really give you a challenge. You're not used to it. I think if you just ride smart you're going to eventually beat him and get that old confidence back. Hell, two races don't make a season."

Mike sighed. "Well, I'll do my best. One consolation is that Mom would sure be happy if I didn't make it to the pros."

"You got that right. Let's see if they've got some grub on for us." Bill said as they turned into the Maslak's driveway.

The following Sunday found Mike and Bill at Salmon River in western New York. On the way out, it had started to rain and it was now coming down in a steady drizzle. Motocross was a rain or shine sport and the races would go off as scheduled. Bill had thrown two brand new tires into the van before they left because the forecast had been for rain. Rain meant mud and lots of it. They would work together to put the new tires on before the race. Many riders disliked the mud but Mike ran well in it. Fast, slippery down hills and muddy corners tested everyone's skill. And rain meant no dust.

The pit area blossomed with multicolored umbrellas and all sorts of raingear. Tarps and tents were pitched and riders bundled against the wet and the chill hardly recognized one another as they went about preparing for the race.

The minis and juniors returned from practice with bikes and bodies covered in mud. The track was awash in at least two or three inches of slippery goo. Puddles had become small muddy ponds. It took skill to cross these spots. Six or seven inches of muddy water could hide a foot of mud underneath. The lines changed rapidly also. What was a good line on one lap might suck a rider in the next.

Mike was well aware of all these pitfalls. He was used to riding under any conditions. In fact, he seemed to run better than most riders in mud and rain. Spectators shook their heads in wonder, as Mike would head down a straightaway at breakneck speed, covered in mud, but racing without a care in the world.

"The faster you go, the easier it is." he explained to Bill. And he was right. Wheels on a motorcycle act like a gyroscope. The faster a gyroscope spins, the harder it is to change angles.

Bill was impressed that he knew this. "If I'd only known that twenty years ago. Us flat trackers, though, were much smarter than you guys. We canceled races when it rained," he laughed.

Mike laughed at the memories of some his own tumbles. "Of course we don't always use it just perfect."

"I guess not," Bill said as he rubbed the seat of his pants in memory of a fifty-foot bumpy slide he had taken on his butt during a flat track race.

Mike and Ackley took advantage of the full practice period for the 250's. Mike tried to stay away from Ackley because he knew he would be following and he didn't want to give Ackley any advantage if he could help it.. Mike decided to go slow, check the track and let Ackley figure out his own lines. Ackley discovered this early and passed Mike, "roosting" or spraying him with as much mud and rocks as he could.

With Ackley out of the way, Mike started to experiment and found that most of the lines he had liked in the past were still basically the same. He pulled back into the pits, took off his mud splattered helmet and rain suit and smiled at Bill. "Man, it's slippery. I'm glad we put those new tires on. But I feel great. Ackley, here I come!"

"That's the stuff," Bill replied. "Go out there and nail his hide to the wall. You can do it."

Mike put his hand on Bill's shoulder "Nobody beats this team today." He said with a grin.

Under a large umbrella, the two watched as the other races went off. Occasionally, a friend or fan of Mike's stopped to say hello. Without exception, they all urged him to beat Ackley. They were very disturbed over what had happened to Tony.

"You can do it, Mike." One said. "Man, I saw you run in the mud at East Hill last year. You were unbelievable. Some of those clowns were falling on their faces and you just kept motoring as if the sun was out."

Mike thanked him for his support and told him he would try. The truth was, he loved compliments about his riding skill and he really did feel good about today. He could ride well in the slop. He knew it and the other riders, including Ackley, knew it too. His running every morning gave him more confidence in his staying power. No more fading in the last couple of laps, he told himself.

Bill had also given him an extra half hour off from work each afternoon so that he could practice that much more. The truth was, he didn't need to ride that often because he wanted to give tired and aching muscles a chance to heal during the week to be ready for the weekend. Instead, he used the extra time on needed bike maintenance and preparation.

He and Bill watched as the first of the 125's went off. It was time for him to get ready. He changed in the back of the van and moved to the front seat beside Bill. "How was your mother this week?"

"Ok, I guess, still not happy with my racing."

"Damn, just what you need with the National at Unadilla right around the corner. Try not to think about it right now. We'll see if we can hatch some strategy to bring her around on the way home. By the way, we've got to send in for your entry and pro license pretty quick."

"Bill, I've been meaning to talk to you about that. Tell me honestly, do you really think I'm ready?. Ackley has been really doing a job on me."

Bill looked at him incredulously. "Ready, ready?" he almost screamed. "You've never looked better. My God you're flying

Charles Loomis

out there. Ackley's a flash in the pan. You've got him so spooked he can hardly stand up let alone ride a bike. You can't see it from where you are but he's dying out there. He's a load, no finesse at all. He just muscles his way around and is dead by the end of the race. He can't hold a candle to you. Everyone knows it, everyone says it. He's no problem, you'll take him today, hands down."

"Still," Mike said tentatively.

"Still nothin'. You're going out there and beat Ackley today and we're going to the nationals."

"OK, you've got me convinced. Let me at him." Mike said brightly, changing the mood.

"Don't get smart," Bill laughed. "I'm not through with you yet. Let me tell you something. An athlete's biggest enemy is from his shoulders on up. You better not get discouraged about Ackley because you're going to face a lot better, smarter and tougher riders when you get to the nationals. Those guys didn't get there worrying about the first guy that gave them a real run for their money. You've go to get over that, Mike. Face each challenge as it comes. And I'll tell you something, else, the challenges get tougher the older you get. There's always Ackley's waiting around to skin your hide right off you. Why hell, you're somebody else's Ackley."Look at Jim Turner. He's a nice guy, but he's going to take you down the first chance he gets."

Motocross Mike

Mike was quiet for a moment. "I really hadn't thought about Jim Turner that way. It must be tough to run third all the time. Jeez, fourth when Tony is running. He's probably hoping we all go pro and leave district three to him."

"You can bet he'd love that. He's been running behind you and Tony his whole life but he still hangs in there."

"You're right as usual, Bill. But Mom is still a tough problem. It really bugs me. I hate doing something that I know hurts her so much."

"Yeah, me too. I think an awful lot of that gal, I hate to see her suffer. We'll have to work on that even though Janice says I should keep my hands off and let you and your Mom work it out. Well, whaddaya say, Buddy, let's get down to business."

While they were talking, Mike had been inserting "tear offs" in front of the lenses on his goggles. In severe mud conditions, they were absolutely necessary. When one layer of plastic muddied, a tab pulled it away until it got muddy and was, in turn, discarded. Five or six could be inserted over the lenses and when they were gone, riders took the chance of throwing away or pulling down their goggles, thereby losing a lot of confidence in following other riders closely. In this situation, the chances of eye injury from rocks and dirt flying off the rear tire of the man in front of you were very great.

Charles Loomis

The trick was to make sure you pulled the right tab when you wanted a clean view. There is upper and lower left and upper and lower right and in a hot contest it's easy to forget which one is next. Mike smiled as he remembered watching an international race at Unadilla and seeing a rider pull the wrong tab while coming off a jump and fill the air with pieces of plastic flying behind him.

The crowd laughed and happily cheered his mistake.

Since he had a change of clothes, Mike decided to run without rain gear. His strategy was to get in front and stay there so he didn't have to worry about flying mud until he passed the lappers. If anybody did get in front of him he'd take his chances and worry about it then.

Bill and he donned rubberized nylon ponchos and made their way to the line for the gate. He drew his number. It was a middle one. The conditions were so wet that it didn't make much difference anyway. He found a decent place on the line and sat on his bike to wait. He watched as Bill cleared the groove for his start position with his booted foot. The ooze filled in again almost as soon as Bill cleared it. He looked at Mike with a gesture of despair. Bill leaned up close to his helmet. "Here we are, two kids playing in the mud," They both laughed.

Ackley, five riders down the line from Mike, watched the two of them.

Motocross Mike

Mike caught Ackley's eyes for just an instant and turned away. He looked up the course at the sky. It was gray with not a trace of the sun. That contrasted with the gay and laughing crowd gathered along the fences of the start area. Pretty girls under multicolored umbrellas and pieces of plastic leaned against their boyfriends. He smiled. Motocross fans are great; they'll party in any kind of weather.

Bill nudged him and he looked up to see the starter headed for his position.

The 125 experts were coming off the track. He started his bike and Bill slid the poncho off over his head. Bill said he would hold it over his head until the last seconds and then turn his back on the deluge of mud and rocks that would get hurled back at him on the start.

The card was up on the two-minute position. He brought his concentration to bear on the track entrance, willing himself there. The starter turned it to "one" and each rider twisted the throttle on his bike more frantically. The board went sideways, the gate dropped and they were off. Mike's new rear tire bit hard into the mud and chewed down to solid dirt. He rocketed out of the start. It wasn't fast enough. Ackley was ahead of him. He stayed right on Ackley's back wheel waiting for him to make a mistake. Ackley was all over the track, right on the brink of control. Mike couldn't tell whether he was really out of control or simply trying to frustrate him by blocking him from passing. Ackley's erratic path spewed mud and water all over Mike and he already regretted not wearing his rain jacket over his jersey. He released a tear off two hundred yards into the race and dropped back to better observe Ackley in action. Very quickly, he observed that Ackley was out of control most of the time. That was good. It meant he would probably tire quickly.

Mike slid up behind Ackley on the turns, braking at the last possible minute. Ackley knew he was there. He kept trying to turn around so he could see Mike, but he was so busy trying to keep his bike under control in the deepening mud that he couldn't afford to stop concentrating. Mike knew now that he could get by him practically anytime. But thoughts of Tony's broken leg came to him. "Pay back time," he thought.

Ackley knew that Mike was sliding up to him on every corner and he made some attempts to roost Mike in order to throw him off. He struggled to keep his bike under control. Mike on the other hand, had complete control and simply dodged Ackley's feeble moves.

The sodden crowd rose to watch the battle rage in the mud and the rain. They knew that their favorite was in charge. They watched as Mike crowded Ackley into the corners like a cat playing with a mouse, and then backed off to watch Ackley wallow out of them. On one of the muddiest sections, Ackley almost ran over

Motocross Mike

a flagman as he cut the track and went around the section instead of through it as track layout demanded. Mike wheelied straight through. The crowd screamed its approval .

On the last lap, the flagman moved to the edge of the mud hole and pointed with his flag to the route Ackley was supposed to take. Ackley skirted it again and almost ran the flagman down a second time. The flagman fell in the mud trying to get out of his way. Mike wheelied through again.

Mike picked a spot and passed. He literally wheelied by Ackley demonstrating his superior skill. The crowd roared. Remembering the mud bath that Ackley had given him at Royal Mountain, he stayed just far enough ahead of him to thoroughly cover him and then shot away to cross the finish line twenty yards in the lead.

Bill met Mike at the track exit. He hopped on behind Mike and they made their way to the pits with Bill yelling in his ear over the noise of the crowd, "I said you could do it. I told you so you son of a gun," over and over.

Back at the van, Mike peeled off his wet, muddy clothing as his fans gathered around, cheering and congratulating him. Over and over he heard how terrific he was and "What a ride. Perfect, Mike, perfect."

Mike was glad. He had changed into dry clothes and a warm jacket after sponging off the mud. He only wished Tony

Charles Loomis

could have been there to savor the first moto with him. But Mike reminded himself that he had another moto to go before the day was a complete success. Startled, he looked up to see Ackley staring down at him.

"I'll never forget what you did to me today. You better not ever let me catch you out without your friends around you."

Mike stared back. "Lighten up, will ya, fella? You only got what you asked for. You seem to be able to dish it out much better than you can take it."

"I'll show you how to take it next moto, hotshot. You better watch out," he said threateningly as he turned away.

Bill came around the side of the van shaking his head. Ackley had not seen him. "Man, if you could harness the meanness in that kid, you'd have some machine."

"That's for sure." Mike said as he sipped hot coffee out of a thermos.

Mike peered around the side of the van. He watched Ackley fifty feet away shoving, someone. He recognized the flagman.

"Look at this! Now he's pushing the flagman around because he wouldn't let him cut the course!."

"Well, I'll be damned! The kid probably makes two bucks an hour and all the hot dogs he can eat. I don't believe this guy."

Mike watched to make sure no physical harm came to the flagman and then sat back down. A plan was taking shape in his

Motocross Mike

mind--one that he didn't tell Bill about. He knew Bill would be too concerned for his safety to let him do it.

The second 250 expert moto started without problems. The rain was still coming down, but everyone was resigned to it. This time Mike had the hole shot and he held the lead for a lap before letting Ackley go by. He faked a slip on a turn in front of the area with the largest crowd. Ackley had to pass him or look foolish. Mike slipped up behind Ackley a little to the side so that his roost wouldn't get him. As they approached the mud hole they were supposed to go through, Ackley moved to go around it, pushing Mike up with him.

The flagman was well out of the way as the two bikes climbed the slight embankment around the slop. Mike waited until they were right next to the deepest part and suddenly gassed his bike around in front of Ackley, veering back into the mud hole as if he had made a mistake. It happened exactly as he planned. Ackley was surprised and momentarily lost his balance, slithering down into the hole as Mike motored away.

When he looked around, all he could see was a handlebar sticking up, Ackley sitting in the mud and one happy flagman jumping around.

Mike crossed the finish line. Ackley was nowhere to be seen. Mike greeted the cheering crowd with a fist in the air. He had won his first race of the season.

Charles Loomis

Wet and tired, he plopped down in a lawn chair near the van and held an umbrella over his head. His smile said it all. Happy fans came through the flimsy fence around the pits and surrounded Mike. They walloped him on the back and shoulder pads and some hugged him as he struggled to his feet under the onslaught. They were jumping around hooting and yelling when suddenly a voice boomed out.

"I won't forget what you did to me, Porter." Ackley screamed as he advanced on Mike. Mike squared his shoulders, ready for the worst He was ready to defend himself.

"Ackley, you asked for it." he said

Suddenly, out of the crowd came Chub Smith. Chub was taller than Mike and Ackley and outweighed them by about forty pounds. The crowd hushed as Chub moved between Ackley and Mike.

He placed his big hands on Ackley's shoulders and very quietly but distinctly said to him, "You want Mike on the track, that's OK. Off the track you got to go through me first. You got that fella?" He gave Ackley a shove that put him on his back in the mud.

Ackley quickly got to his feet and started moving away. Over his shoulder he yelled and swore at Mike. Chub ran towards him and Ackley fell again. Chub pulled up short and stifled a laugh as Ackley got to his feet and scrambled to his van.

Motocross Mike

"I don't think he'll be bothering you again. What do you think Mike?"

Mike was glad to see his friend. "Where did you come from? I didn't even know you were here."

Chub smiled at his friend. "Well, can't work in the rain so thought I'd shoot over here to see you win your first race. Nice work, ol' Pal."

"Thanks Chub. You know, I could have handled Ackley. I was ready to put a couple of my best wrestling moves on him."

Chub laughed. "Were you going to do that after he beat your brains in or before?"

Mike laughed as the two friends clapped each other on the back and made their way to Bill's van.

Chub helped Mike and Bill load up. They slowly made their way out of the muddy pit area with Chub following close behind in his car.

CHAPTER SIXTEEN

On the way home, the three friends stopped at their favorite restaurant in Syracuse. After they ordered dinner, Mike and Bill headed for the nearest pay phone. They couldn't wait to tell Mario and Tony the news. .

"You did real good, Mike – fantastic," Mario said.

Tony got on the extension phone. As Mike told the story again, Tony kept asking, "and then what happened, and then what happened?"

At last, Mike handed the phone to Bill. He told them how Ackley had gotten stuck in the pit area in his van after the race and no one would help him. He finally had to call a tow truck.

"The last time we saw him he was kicking his van and cursing Mike, motocross and life in general. The guy was going berserk! He'll either never show his face in District Three again, or he'll come back a changed person."

Motocross Mike

They said their goodbyes. Mike and Bill returned to Chub and their dinner. Happily, they recapped the day and made plans for the future.

Back in the van, Mike slept soundly. Bill smiled all the way home.

The following Sunday, at Hammondtown Ackley did show up, only to have Mike trounce him once more. He seemed to fly around the sandy track, always making Ackley work to the maximum. Mike's training paid off handsomely. He was hardly winded between motos.

Local races were usually eight or ten laps, depending on the length of the track. That usually meant each moto ran about twenty minutes. Pro races, on the other hand, were forty minutes long plus two laps per moto. Anticipating the possibility of going pro, Mike extended his practice periods to forty minutes.

The weather turned warmer. Ackley was obviously bushed between motos. He said nothing to Mike and stayed away from him. On the track he followed Mike as closely as he could, but found that he just couldn't match Mike's blistering pace. All he could do was sit back and wait for Mike to make a mistake or suffer a mechanical problem. Mike amazed the spectators with his riding skill. His jumps were long and high. His wheelies over the bumps always controlled. His cornering was stupendous as he playfully roosted the spectators sending plumes of dirt arching

Charles Loomis

from his back wheel. Ackley tried to follow suit but just couldn't cut it.

For close racing, the spectators had to watch Jim Turner and others battle for third or fourth. There was a pack of five or six riders seeking those positions every week. They always provided some fast, interesting competition, in contrast Mike's effortless style.

The fans began to ask Mike when he would announce he was going "pro".

Mike's reply was always the same. "We'll see.". The truth was, he didn't want to fuel any rumors until he'd worked things out with his mother. It was going to be difficult. Graduation was only a couple of weeks away and his mother had been admonishing him for not applying to any colleges as yet.

"Don't worry Mom, with my average and SAT scores I won't have any problems finding a school."

She knew he was avoiding the issue.

One day, she confronted Bill at the shop. "Are you and Mike plotting on the side to get around me?" she asked.

"What do you mean?" he said with a puzzled look.

"Oh, come on Bill. I know you want Mike to race pro instead of going to college. It's obvious."

Motocross Mike

Bill sighed."Look, Ann, I've told you before. I think you're making a mistake, but I'm keeping my nose out of this. It's something you and Mike have to work out yourselves."

"You might consider trying to help him understand my side."

"You might not believe this, but I have. You know how I felt about Mike Sr. – how I feel about you. You and he have been Janice's and my best friends. Because I think you're making a mistake on this one issue doesn't change that. You've done a heck of a job raising that kid. I just think it's time you turned him loose a little. Give him some choices; let him explore something that he's very good at. I used to get more nervous watching that kid wrestle than I ever did watching him race" He paused looking intently into Ann Porter's eyes.. "Sorry, " He went on. "I've already said more than I was going to. I'm not saying anymore."

Mike was very much aware that he was the cause of a great deal of friction between his mother and Bill and it weighed heavily on his mind. Privately, he devised a plan.

Two weeks later, on a Saturday morning Bill came back in the shop area with a large manila envelope addressed to Mike.

"Hey ," he called excitedly. "You've got something here from the American Motorcyclist Association. It looks important."

"Thanks Bill," Mike answered carefully. "Just leave it on my workbench."

Bill studied him for a long moment. "Hey kid, I don't want to say anything but the National is only two weeks away. You've got to make up your mind. I haven't said much because I'm in enough trouble with your mother already."

Mike glanced up, his eyes twinkling. "Well, maybe you should open the envelope then."

Bill opened the envelope and examined the contents. It was Mike's pro license and two mechanic's licenses. He looked at Mike, a little bewildered. "Who did this?" he asked.

Mike gave a shrug. "I did. I figured it was about time I made some decisions on my own without putting you in the middle."

"Alright! We're going to the nationals," Bill whooped. "Hey, wait a minute, where'd you get the money for this? I'm the sponsor. If you laid out for this it's up to me to reimburse you."

"I got it from my savings. We'll talk about that later. First of all I want Mom to know that I did it on my own. I'd like to go to the national with her support if I can."

"Well, like I said, that's between you and your Mom."

CHAPTER SEVENTEEN

That night, Mike went home to face his mother. He found her in the living room, reading and sat down next to her, a little nervously.

"Mom," he began quietly. "Before you hear it from someone else, I got my pro license today."

She turned to look at him a stunned look on her face. " I knew it! I knew you and Bill were up to something!" Tears welled up in her eyes.

He took her hand gently in his. "Mom, look at me. I said I got the license. Bill didn't know anything about it until it came in the mail today."

"You're just covering up for him!."

"No, I mean it. He hasn't said a word to me about it. He thought you and I had to work it out. I knew it was really getting

Charles Loomis

to him, too. The National's only two weeks from now. But I swear, Mom. He never said a word."

Ann sighed in exasperation. "So now you're telling me that this decision to run is all yours, even though you know how I feel about it?"

"Yes."

"Oh Michael, how could you?" The tears now spilled down her cheeks.

"Mom, please don't cry. You don't know how much it hurts me. Listen I'm a big boy now. I can make decisions on my own."

"No matter what it does to your mother?"

"That's not it. I want to do this with your help and support. I need that, Mom."

"To race a national and splatter your brains all over the track. You need me for that? No thanks. Seeing one person I loved die on a racetrack is enough."

"Mom, please!"

"Your father didn't need me there to do that." A burst of sobs came from deep in her chest.

"Mom, how many times do I have to tell you that motocross is relatively safe? Nobody dies and there are only a very few crippling injuries."

Motocross Mike

"That's what you keep telling me. But remember, statistics don't matter when you're the one involved. Besides, look at what happened to your pal, Tony"

"So you've made up your mind? You're not going to change it?"

Mike was three inches taller than his mother but she never looked taller than when she looked up at him straight in the eye and said, "No!" With that, she angrily left the room.

Mike threw himself into a chair. He'd fully expected to wear her down in the end. He wasn't prepared for this. Her rejection of his racing made him heartsick.

His head was spinning with conflicting thoughts. If only Dad were alive, he'd be able to explain. Somehow he knew his father would be on his side.. On the other hand, his death racing motorcycles was the cause of the conflict in the first place.

Mike's mind raced. Part of him said, "Forget motocross, nothing's worth seeing my mother like this." While another part of him insisted. "Why is she standing in the way of something I love so much? "

He stood up tiredly. "Why can't I have a family that supports me?" he said to the empty room. " If I do it anyway, I can't even enjoy it. Not if I'm breaking Mom's heart."

He glanced toward the light still burning in the kitchen and headed up the stairs. The truth was, he didn't know what to do.

Charles Loomis

The next morning over breakfast, his mother was the first to break the silence. "Michael, if you're bound and determined to do this anyway, maybe it would be a good idea for me to just take a vacation until it's over. I need one anyway. I could go to the shore for a couple of weeks and you and Bill can concentrate on the race without me interfering."

Mike stared at her. "Oh Mom, please. Can't you just stick with me on this.? You'll see, it'll be okay," he pleaded.

Ann Porter raised a skeptical eyebrow. "That's unfair Mike." she replied. " I've stuck with you on everything in your life until now. I just can't stand to see you take this risk."

"I'm sorry, Mom. You've got me so mixed up I don't know what I'm saying."

"That's why it's better if I go. That way you can concentrate on your racing. At least, I want you fully prepared. You can stay with the Maslaks. I'll leave in the morning."

"Mom, please don't go."

"Are you going to race?"

"Yes."

"Then I'm going. You said you were a big boy and can take care of yourself, so, I'm going."

That was the end of it. Mike knew it and so did she. Both were locked into their own decisions. Mike would stay with the Maslaks until after the nationals. She would go to the shore until it was over. Or, as she feared, Mike wound up in the hospital. Or worse.

Mike, Bill and Janice saw her off the next morning. "Jeez Ann, come on. Don't you want to be there when Mike wins his first national?" Bill said plaintively.

Ann eyed him, a little coldly. "I really don't. Because you know as well as I do--if he wins this one he'll just want to race the next one."

Bill stuck his head through the car window and kissed Ann on the cheek. "Hey, it doesn't have to be this way. You ought to be there."

"Bill, please, it'll be better this way."

As she pulled out of the driveway, Mike felt his chest tighten. "Mom?"

She stuck her head out the window. "Yes?" she asked hopefully.

"Nothing, ": Mike answered. "Have a good time."

She smiled, a little sadly. "You too." she told him. And drove away.

CHAPTER EIGHTEEN

At a little after five-thirty in the morning. Mike and Bill pulled up to the long line of vans, trucks and cars waiting for the pit gate at Unadilla to open. Bill got out of the van and gabbed with the mechanics, riders and team managers, along with just about everyone else involved in the racing scene that he'd met over the years. The scene was a carnival of colors and noise as the riders and their friends joked and chided one another.

Mike chatted with a couple of pro riders that he knew, Steve Sanders and Danny Collins. Steve and Danny were two of the nicest guys on the circuit. Their joking and clowning helped Mike relax. But for the most part, Mike was quiet, trying to soothe his ragged nerves. He was trying to look cool. He didn't want to show everyone this was his first professional race. Neither he nor Bill had slept very well. They had come down to stay with Mario and Tony the night before, and by the time they finished talking it was midnight. Mike had tossed and turned, thinking of the big day. Though he'd had less than three hours of sleep, he didn't feel the least bit tired this morning. His adrenalin was flowing. He eagerly awaited the opening of the pit gate so that he could busy himself preparing for practice, qualifying, and finally, the race itself later that afternoon. The busy schedule of national motocross packed everything into one day.

Mike saw the Honda reps, Hugh Black and Jim Hawkins, making their way over to him. He turned to them and smiled as they reached out to shake Mike's hand.

"From all reports, Mike, it sounds like you're having a good season." Hugh said.

"Hey, how are you guys?" Mike greeted them. "We got off to a slow start but everything seems to be clicking now. I love the new bike. It really hooks up good and handles better than any bike I ever rode."

"We're anxious to see you run today."

Mike laughed. "It's been on my mind, that's for sure."

Hugh and Jim joined in his laughter. "Ok, just concentrate on the race and don't worry about us."

"Thanks, I'll try to do that."

Hugh and Jim again shook hands with Mike. Jim placed his hand on Mike's shoulder. "Well, good luck Mike. We'd really like to see you do well today."

Charles Loomis

Mike waved. "I'll do my best."

Bill returned to urge Mike back into the van. "The line is starting to move, let's go."

They showed their credentials and drove into the pit area, finding a level spot to pitch the tarp they had brought with them to protect them from the sun or in case of unexpected rain.

The pit area remained quiet, with the exception of the "swish, swish, swish" of the huge sprinklers watering the track. The weather had been dry and sprinklers were needed to keep the track moist. Dust was the enemy of both spectators and riders. Limited visibility could cause accidents and injury to riders as well as limit the visibility of spectators.

At one point, Bill stopped and put his arm around Mike's shoulders to give him a quick hug. A huge smile lit up his face.

"What a day Mike! I've been looking forward to this for a long time. Look, kid, no matter what happens today nobody can say that we didn't do our best. There are a lot of tough guys out there. Guys trying to hold on to their professional lives. They won't take kindly to a young upstart like you trying to blow them off the track. If you're fast in practice and qualifying, they'll be looking for you. I'm not saying that you're going to run into another Ackley – they're too smart for that – but they'll be putting on the pressure."

Motocross Mike

The moment wasn't lost on Mike. A wave of affection flooded over him as he realized once more the tremendous gap that Bill filled in his life since the loss of his father.

"Thanks Bill. I never could have gotten here without you. I want you to know how much I appreciate everything you've done. Like you said, no matter what happens today, we're still the best team that anyone ever put together."

Bill was moved. He nodded and coughed a little to disguise his emotion. "Okay. Lets get going. I'll unload and you check the track out."

"Right."

Mike caught up with the riders that he'd talked to that morning. They decided to walk the track together.

"Hey, Mike, " Steve Sanders began in his slow Texas drawl. "Let's walk this thing. We've got to find a good place to bury you."

"Very funny, " Mike answered. " Of course, you guys know that this track is one of my favorites. I know it like the back of my hand. Maybe I'll do some burying myself."

"Ah Ha! The young pup snaps back. Well, I hear you've got a little experience in burying. You tangled with a guy named Ackley up here, right? Some of the guys who have run up against him were pretty happy about that. Couldn't have happened to a nicer guy. Ha Ha!"

Charles Loomis

Mike smiled. "Yeah, we had our differences."

"The young pup is modest, too. How about that, Danny?" He said to the slight red haired rider smiling beside him. "We heard that you put him into a mud hole and buried him, bike and all."

Mike glanced at Steve and smiled. "Gee, now I wouldn't do anything like that, it's against the rules. I was real close to him when it happened and the way I saw it was, he just slipped right down into the biggest, deepest mud hole on the track."

The three young men laughed and continued their way around the track. They checked every hill, turn and straightaway. When they were finished, they went to the start area and checked that out too.

Nobody checked the start area more closely than Mike. He kicked and prodded at the turf and checked the exit of any position he might have on the start line. Unlike the amateur races he was used to, a rider's finish in the qualifying heats determined his position on the start line. Mike had no idea how he would finish, so he wanted to make sure he had all exits covered.

The sun rose in the sky and streamed down on a beautiful summer morning. The colorful crowd milled about the track. The riders killed some time watching the spectators and exchanging words with them now and then along the pit area fence.

The newer riders on the circuit were quieter and more nervous. Most stayed more or less in hiding or around their vans, busying themselves with this and that to kill the time until practice began.

Mike was no exception. After following Danny and Steve to the fence and a couple of glances at the crowd he slipped away.

Mike knew that checking his bike one more time would yield nothing but he did it anyway.

Bill had polished the bright work and plastic on the bike as many times as Mike had but also did it again anyway. They looked at each other and laughed, breaking the tension.

"Mike, if I rub this anymore the numbers will disappear."

Mike nodded. "If I check it one more time I won't have any skin left on my fingers."

"Let's just relax and wait for practice."

Practice started at 9:00 for the 125's. They would be out for about forty-five minutes and then Mike would go out for 250 practice. He pulled on his gear and made sure all adjustments were to his liking and comfort. He stepped to the side of the track to watch the 125's scream by. They sounded like a bunch of bees swarming around a hive.

Mike watched in admiration. The pros seemed to wind them out and shift them anytime they wanted without getting off the gas at all.

125 riders pared their weight down to a bare minimum. The combination of that and the lightness of the 125 bikes made it a fast and fun class to watch as they grouped together flying through the air off the jumps and bumps.

Mike felt his pulse quicken as he watched the action. He ached to be on the track to see how he would fare in the 250 pro class. Most of the other riders were suited up and he recognized some of them from pictures in magazines. Others had names on the backs of their shirts that he knew.

A few riders were like him, trying a pro race for the first time. He wondered if he looked as nervous as they did.

The 250's were called to the line for practice and Mike pushed his bike to the start area. Bill tagged along gawking at the color and feeling the excitement of the big day.

The start area was a mass of men and machines. The riders were outfitted in various team colors. They looked clean and well tailored. Mike knew that would change fast as they were exposed to the dust, dirt, mud and sweat. Some riders lounged against the fence separating the start area from the spectators. Others discussed different parts of the track and race strategy with their mechanics and team managers.

Mike's practice strategy was simple. He would take two laps at a moderate pace to learn the track and check it out, burning the layout into his mind. After that he would go as fast as he could

Motocross Mike

for two or three laps, being careful not to crash. Then he planned to slow down to a moderate pace to reinforce the track's images in his mind. He'd be careful not to burn himself out in practice and qualifying.

The 125's were flagged off the track. When it was clear, the starter let the 250's go in groups of three or four so they wouldn't be bunched together and be tempted to race with one another instead of practice.

Mike was in the middle of the pack and stuck to his resolve not to push too hard until he had studied the track. Even though he'd raced at Unadilla many times as an amateur and an expert, he knew that they made changes to meet the demands of a national or international pro race. Jumps might be added, turns changed or sections added or deleted. He stood on the pegs and studied the track as he made his way around. He let other riders go by while he tried to restrain himself from twisting the throttle on and doing faster laps.

Mike carefully made his way around. Once in a while he could hear the crowd cheer as a favorite pro rode by. He glanced to the sidelines now and then to see the crowd. He was curious, he had never raced in front of so many people. But he resolved not to let the crowd distract him. Instead, he would concentrate on his racing.

Charles Loomis

The big spectator jump was coming up and Mike couldn't resist putting on a small show. He picked up speed and readied himself for the long flight off the lip.

The crowd screamed.. He was high in the air and looking down at the cheering faces as he twisted the bike to the left and then back to the right just before he landed. The crowd cheered his double cross up wildly. He landed and wheelied into the next corner, in complete control. Nearer the fence, he could see clenched fists waving approval to urge him on. A few people hollered, "Go Mike".

And "go" he did. He finished his inspection laps, all the time picking up his pace. Other riders didn't pass him as often now. He got into the rhythm of the track and literally flew through the remainder of practice.

He pulled back into the pits after practice and made his way to the van.

"Let me help you with that," Bill said as Mike hopped off the bike and passed the bars to Bill. "You looked great out there, kid."

Mike was excited. "Bill, I felt great. Did you see me come off the big jump?"

Bill gave him a mock look of disapproval. "Yes I did. Please don't crash, we've got a long day ahead of us."

Motocross Mike

Mike lifted his helmet and smiled.. "Just having a little fun to break the tension."

"Just make sure that's all you break. How did the bike run?"

"Perfect. No problem at all. I wouldn't touch anything before qualifying. Just clean her up, check her out and we'll go."

"OK, go relax. I'll take care of everything."

"Relax? Look at me, Bill, I'm hardly sweating. I've got so much energy left in me I could run a marathon right now and come back and race."

"Save it, kid. Wait until some of the full-time pros start pushing you. We'll see how much energy you've got."

Mike couldn't get the grin off his face. "What a day, huh Bill? I just wish one thing."

"What's that kid?"

"I just wish Mom was here."

"I know kid, I know. But try not to think about it. Just concentrate on the race. Believe me, she'll be excited if you do well - especially if you come out without a scratch. So please, no more fancy jumps, OK?"

"OK, Bill, you got it. No more fancy stuff, just go fast and don't fall."

"Now you're talking. We'll show them the meaning of the word 'preparation'. Now go sit down and I'll check the bike out."

Charles Loomis

Mike sat on the back of the van and watched Bill go over the bike. He was relaxed and happy. Everything is going great, he thought. After a moment, he spotted a loose nut and pointed it out to Bill. Before long the two friends were deeply involved with the bike.

Without warning, Mike felt a presence at his back. He turned his head and looked up into the smiling face of his mother.

"Mom!" he yelled.

Bill turned to look and dropped the wrench out of his hand. "Ann, what the ----, " He stood with his mouth open watching Mike and his mother hugging each other. "I thought you were at the shore."

"I just couldn't stay away.", Ann answered as tears streamed down her face.

Bill gaped at her. "I didn't think you'd change your mind for anything. You don't know how much difference this will make to Mike. This is a wonderful, wonderful day."

"Mom, I love you!" Mike joined in happily. " I never once thought you'd change your mind. This is great. I'm so happy. I'm going to make you very proud of me today."

"Just do your best, Hon, I'm already proud of you."

Mike held his mother at arms length. "Wow, Mom, you look great with that tan. You must have had some good weather."

Ann smiled. "I did a lot of thinking on the beach, Mike. I decided I just couldn't stand in the way of anything you love so much."

"But Mom, how did you get into the pits?" Mike asked his mother.

"It's not like I'm a complete stranger to the circuit, Mike. The track owners gave me a guest pass.

Mike hugged his mother again and Bill put his arm around her.

"This is a great day, Ann. Fantastic!" he said. He shook his head and moved away. "But I've got to get back to work."

CHAPTER NINETEEN

Mike waited patiently for his qualifying session to begin. He chatted quietly with his mother after he and Bill had carefully gone over every part of the bike.

The day was perfect, the sun was warm and careful track preparation kept the dust down. The three of them watched as the 125's ran their qualifying heats. Twenty disappointed riders pulled off the track as only the first ten of the thirty who entered are chosen in each qualifying heat.

The riders, who had been clean and fresh faced at the start, were now sweat soaked, their faces streaked with grime. Their clothes and boots were caked with mud from the wetter parts of the track. The shiny racing bikes were now caked with mud and dirt.

Motocross Mike

Those that didn't qualify would have one more race to try to make the big race before the day was over. This was called a consolation race.

Mike wanted to clinch a start position on his first try to conserve his strength for the main race of the day. When they called for the 250s, he was ready.

Once again, they pushed the bike to the start area and Mike readied himself for his qualifying moto.

He threw his leg over his bike and heaved a sigh. "Well, here we go,

Bill, my first pro qualifier."

"You'll do well, kid. Don't let them spook you. Just qualify. Don't kill yourself, just qualify. Remember, all you need to do is to place in the top ten. And even if you don't -there's always the consolation qualifier. But I have the feeling we won't need that today," Bill said with a wink.

Mike smiled at Bill. "Don't worry, we're going to be right up there."

Bill patted Mike on the back and picked up his chalkboard and small tool bag that he always carried when Mike was on the track. He then made his way to the mechanics area. Mechanics were not allowed to wander around the track and were confined to a designated area where they could flash their chalkboards with information about the race to their rider. The messages would tell the rider such things as what place he was in, when to speed up or slow down, if another rider was overtaking him, or if he was in the clear and how much time was left in the race.

Mike settled in at the start line and watched as the board turned and his group was off. He was in the first five to hit the entrance turn onto the track. He was running comfortably. He picked up two more places almost immediately and then settled in behind two veteran riders, Steve Sanders and Mike Buel. Since he wasn't out to prove anything during the qualifier, he decided to stick with the two more experienced riders and "go to school" on them, so to speak.

He duplicated the lines of the two experienced pro riders around the track for five laps. The pace was steady and much to Mike's liking. He even styled a bit and showed his front wheel to second place Buel once in a while.

The ride was uneventful. Mike exited the track behind the two leaders. He looked relatively fresh and clean, as he had been able to stay out of the thick of the battle. He rode into his pit area, jumped off his bike and heaved it up on the stand. He saw his mother coming at him with her arms outstretched and he turned to catch her in a hug. They laughed as his mother helped him take off his gear.

Bill came huffing into the area. He danced around Mike congratulating him on a good ride.

Motocross Mike

"You did good, kid, real good." he said. "I thought you were going to try to pass those guys in front of you but you used your head and just stayed with them."

A big smile lit up Mike's face. "Yeah, we're in the race, Bill – for sure. You know, I thought I would learn a lot from them but they missed a lot of good lines out there. They knew I was right behind them and I'm positive they were trying to mislead me. I've got all those good lines spotted, Bill, and we'll use them when we get in the race."

"Good thinking. So what do you think about your boy now, Ann?"

"I'm thrilled. You really looked good out there, Mike. I'm still very nervous but I'm glad that you're happy. You know what? I'm happy too."

The three laughed together. Then Mike and Bill cleaned and checked the bike one last time in preparation for the first moto.

Over near the van, Mike leaned back and looked at "his family". At that moment, there wasn't another place on earth he wanted to be. Buel and Sanders ambled over and shook Mike's hand.

"Hey, you looked good out there, rookie," Buel said.

Mike smiled. "I tried. I just couldn't let you guys get too far out in front, you know. I had to show the home folks that us eastern riders can stick with the western boys."

Charles Loomis

"You done good, kid," Sanders said as he patted Mike on the shoulder. "I picked up the pace a bit a couple of times and you hung right in there."

"I noticed. Once I thought my brakes were dragging when you leaped out ahead. Anything you want to tell us about that factory motor you've got there would sure be appreciated." Mike said with a grin.

"After the race we'll tell you anything you want to know, Yankee." Sanders said over his shoulder as he and Buel walked away with big smiles on their faces.

Bill and Mike laughed and turned back to Mike's bike.

"Looks good, Mike."

"Yeah, I don't think I hurt a thing. It ran good and handled like it was on rails. It did everything I wanted it to."

The three moved to the fence to watch the next qualifier. Every once in a while the proud Bill would give Mike a pat on the arm or a look. He nudged Mike.

"Hey Mike, check out the crowd across the track. Some of them are trying to get your attention."

Mike looked out at them and acknowledged each wave or yell with a grin or thumbs up sign. The crowd was dressed for summer and many sat on blankets and lawn chairs soaking up the sun and enjoying the races.

Motocross Mike

Suddenly, he realized that the 125cc. moto was starting and soon it would be his turn to go to the line for the first of his two motos. In his mind, he found himself going over every twist, turn and hill on the rough and tough course.

Mike rolled the bike to the start line for the start of the first moto. Having come in third in the qualifier, he had the third pick for a spot on the start line. He chose a spot on the line near the middle to give him a clear shot at the turn onto the track. Bill left to go to the mechanics area and Mike was left to concentrate on the race ahead.

CHAPTER TWENTY

The starter took his place in front of the riders. Mike concentrated hard on him. The board went sideways and they were off. He had a good start, but was jostled a little by a rider who was temporarily out of control. He backed off the throttle to straighten the bike out and watched in dismay as six riders took advantage of the bobble and beat him to the track entrance.

His careful observance of the good lines on the track paid off now. He whaled the bike into the first turn, a wide sweeper. He took the turn like a flat tracker –sideways with one foot down, lots of power and speed and dirt flying high from his spinning back wheel. Most of the riders slowed to stay to the inside and struggled to keep their bikes upright on the off camber inside line. Mike came out of the turn in fourth place behind Sanders, Buel and another rider. He had gained two places with that one move. He was on the gas and feeling good.

Motocross Mike

He dogged the rider ahead of him. Mike again didn't want Buel and Sanders to get too far into the lead. He wanted to stay near them. He stayed close to the rider ahead of him, hanging on his rear wheel.

They freight trained through the "S" turn before the straight, leading into "Gravity Cavity", a deep gully that dropped the riders down some forty feet, then just as abruptly shot them up and out over the opposite bank in high, long flights of fifty or more feet. Mike's confidence was high as he smiled again as he drew up beside the rider in front of him and they both hit the down slope of the Cavity together. He felt the g-forces as he rocketed up the other side and launched off into the air. In practice and qualifying he had been cautious and had not gotten the height he had now. The pressure of the competition had pushed him and his machine to his limit. Now, he called upon all the skill he had . Flying through the air, he shut the throttle down so as not to over rev the engine. He heard the crowd screaming at him as he looked down at them.

He thought he should be scared. It was the longest and highest jump he had taken in his life. But he wasn't scared at all.. He knew what Bill meant now when he had told him that skill and confidence are both a result of high quality practice. He felt his grin spread over his face as he passed another rider in mid-air. He was cool and confident. He moved his body back on the machine, balancing it so he would land smoothly on both wheels. He had seen many riders go over the handlebars or barely save the bike from bad landings off a jump like this.

Mike landed and had the power on just before the front wheel touched the ground. He kept the bike in a low wheelie to get maximum traction on the back wheel, the front wheel touching the ground just enough to maintain direction until he got to the tight, right turn leading to the back portion of the track. He stuck his right foot out as far as he could reach and laid the bike hard over into the turn without backing off on the throttle. The bike lurched and slid to the bottom of the berm on the outside of the turn. It slammed into the berm almost bottoming out the suspension.

A twenty foot plume of dirt flew from the bike. Mike slipped the clutch to keep the engine revs up while he negotiated the turn. He hit the short straight and pitched into another "s" curve.

Now the back section beckoned. Mike powered through the stadium turn and concentrated on the riders ahead of him, trying not to lose ground. Every inch he gave up would be an inch that he would have to go twice as fast to make up.

They were approaching the "stair steps". This was one of the oldest surviving sections of the track. In the twenty years it had been in existence, it was known to be one of the toughest motocross sections in the world. Bikes had to take huge leaps and maintain speed in an uphill section over big bumps.

Motocross Mike

Mike approached it and measured it with a practiced eye. He knew he was going to have to blip the throttle on and off without letting the RPM's drop too low. He was going to have to hit each one just right and not get bogged down in the heaps of dirt that built up there during a race.

He hit it at speed and nailed the throttle. The bike leapt up the first step and he twisted the throttle on and off over the next steps in precision. Again, he heard the crowd as he negotiated the difficult piece of track.

He now headed for the next challenge – a gradual uphill followed almost immediately by an ultra steep downhill with an abrupt hairpin turn that sent the riders back up the hill. He could see the two leaders just ahead of him. He was determined not to let them get too far ahead, not to lose any ground at all. He felt a sense of satisfaction that he was in third place in his first professional race.

Suddenly the first hill loomed in front of him. Tough, ragged whoopdiedoos scarred the face of the hill from years of motocross bikes ripping and tearing at it. He kept his momentum up and launched off from each bump as he progressed up the hill. A stall would mean he might have to go back down to the bottom and get another run at the difficult terrain. But he held it and cleared the top. He saw the second place rear wheel as it disappeared over the brink of the hill. He slowed to get set for the steep descent down the steepest hill on the course.

He gassed it at the top and heard the spectators scream. He flew down the hill touching just in time to get both brakes on and prevent himself from crashing into the trees at the bottom. He down shifted and gassed the bike hard, twisting it around the hairpin. It leaped off the turn and rocketed up the hill in a high pitched whine. Mike hit the lip and launched himself and the bike skyward.

He landed and powered off, trying to overtake the riders in front of him. He had gained a couple of bike lengths on second place. Buel was right ahead of him.

Mike rode as hard as he had ever ridden before. The seasoned pro on the bike ahead of him was using every trick in the book to keep Mike behind him. Mike could only hope that Buel, who was a former national champion, might begin to tire and allow Mike to slip by.

His muscles were beginning to protest when Bill held up the half way signal on the board. He had only to hold on and press for twenty minutes more.

Sweat began to run down into Mike's goggles and burn into his eyes. He had the urge to rip them off to feel the clean breeze, but that was only asking for trouble. Both Buel and Sanders were throwing up rocks and dirt that he just couldn't dodge. On some

Motocross Mike

corners he felt them fly against his helmet and chest protector with a loud whacking sound. For once, he was glad he wore a lot of padding. His clean pants and jersey were sweat and mud stained. He felt a stinging, burning sensation in his left hand - a direct hit from a large rock..

Still he hung on, waiting for a chance to pass the two riders ahead of him. He knew they were tiring too. He could see them making a few more mistakes on each lap they rode. Yet experience and skill were like a sixth sense to them. They knew just how sloppy they could get in their attempts to ease tired muscles. They also knew how not to let the intruder get by. Each time Mike saw a door around them open, they would snap it shut just before he could make a move.

Five minutes to go. Mike was suddenly aware that a rider who had been gaining on the three leaders was now close behind him. It drew Mike's attention away from the two leaders. He had to close the door on his own pursuer. Mike smiled as he thought how happy Buel and Sanders would be when they knew that someone was keeping him busy.

Mike concentrated on keeping third position. On tight turns he looked back and discovered it was Danny Collins. He hadn't thought about him until now. "He must have had trouble, " Mike thought. "otherwise, he would have been running in the front pack with us." He knew Danny was good. He would have to fight hard to keep him behind.

Mike tried different lines to try to confuse Collins. If Mike went high, Collins stayed low. If Mike went wide riding the berm, Danny fought his bike around the inside, trying to shorten his route to cancel out Mike's speed. Mike concentrated as hard as he could on speed. He rode like a madman for about two laps.

The speed increase brought him close to the leaders once more.. His heart soared when he saw Collins slow down and pull off the track, obviously a victim of mechanical problems.

Mike was relieved and could now concentrate on the two riders ahead of him. He passed the mechanics area and saw Bill giving him the slow down signal. Bill was advising Mike to be happy with a third place finish. He glanced behind him and saw that no bikes were close to challenging him. He decided to resume his cat and mouse game. He did not want to miss any opportunities to pass.

Buel and Sanders played the same game with Mike that he had played with Collins. He knew the sweet feel of being in front and he wanted it in the worst way. It was so much easier to be in front.. All you had to do was concentrate on going as fast as you could and keep closing those doors. Out in front, there were no flying rocks and dirt to contend with until you started to pass the

Motocross Mike

lapped riders. No one knew how hard it is to pass a rider almost as fast as yourself.

Sometimes riders waited half the race to make a move on someone they had raced against before. Sometimes a pass would be made at twice the speed of the overtaken, and the overtaking rider just hangs on and hopes his luck doesn't run out. Braking into a corner is also a prime place to pass. It's why brakes are so important on a motocross bike. The one who can brake in the shortest distance gets to, and through, the corner the fastest. Motocross fans watch for these attempts and laugh as some riders plow right through the berm trying to catch their opponents. Good riders practice that move over and over.

Mike wanted that first place bad but he was smart enough not to take a chance on falling and perhaps coming in last. He was content with third in his first professional outing. Besides, who knew what would happen in the second moto.

He took the checkered flag in third place and turned into the pits. He waved at his screaming and yelling friends and rode his bike to the van in the pit area. His mother greeted him with a smile and helped him lift the bike onto the stand. To Mike it felt like it weighed a ton.

He whipped his helmet and gloves off and collapsed into a nearby lawn chair. His hair hung in wet wisps around his dirty,

Charles Loomis

sweat streaked face. He couldn't remember ever being so tired after a race.

His mother handed him a clean wet towel and a cup of water. He gasped his thanks and swallowed the cool liquid. She took the towel and gently wiped the sweat out of his eyes, then draped the cool towel over his head.

He was finally able to speak. "Thanks, Mom. That really feels good. Well, what do you think?"

"Sweetheart, I'm so thrilled. I always knew you were good, but I just didn't think you would come in third in your first national race. I feel so foolish that I made things so difficult for you. You looked so competent and, and," she stammered, "grown up out there."

Mike smiled at his mom, then reached out and squeezed her arm. "Hey Mom, no sweat. I'm lucky to have a mother who worries so much about me."

She looked at Mike and her eyes shown. She touched his cheek. "How I wish your father was here."

Bill came puffing up the pit road carrying his tool kit and chalkboard. Ann and Mike laughed at his red face and excitement. He was almost dancing.

"Fantastic – super ride", he blurted out. "I hung on that third like a dog with a big bone. You had Buel and Sanders twisting around to look for you so often that I thought they were going to fall off."

He stuck out his hand to Mike. "Congratulations, Mike, you done yourself proud."

Mike smiled and shook Bill's hand. "You helped, 'ol buddy. I could never have done it without you."

"What a kid, what a kid, eh Ann?" Bill said as he grabbed her hands and twirled her in a jig as passers-by laughed at the happy scene.

CHAPTER TWENTY-ONE

Bill began to prepare the bike for the second moto as Mike slowly recovered from the exhaustion of the first. Mike stripped down to the bathing suit he wore under his gear and poured water over his head, soaped up and washed as good as he could under the circumstances. He felt like he was wearing a hundred pounds of mud.

He dried himself and slipped on his sneakers and a light jacket. He sat watching Bill and his mother. The warm bright sun bored into his tired muscles, relaxing him. He had never felt better in his whole life, he thought, as he sat watching his little "family" working to help him.

He was proud of himself and wondered if the factory reps had been watching him race. He got out of the chair and stepped over to where his mother was polishing his goggles and cleaning the caked dirt and mud off his motocross boots.

"Mom, you don't have to do that. I'll take are of it as soon as I rest up."

She smiled up at him. "That's OK, Hon, I want to be part of the team too, you know. You just concentrate on the race. Bill and I will make sure everything is all set for you."

Mike laughed. "You guys are great. " he said, "I can't help but do well with a team like you."

Mike lay down in the back of the van and closed his eyes. He needed to gather his strength for the second moto – the one that he believed would start him down a new path as a professional motocross racer. For years he had dreamed of crisscrossing the country, racing on all the tracks and in all the stadiums he had read about in Motocross Action and Cycle World. He looked forward to meeting and having fun with the top riders and seeing how the top teams operated and examining the exotic equipment that they rode.

Many great riders rode stock, out-of-the-box bikes. A skillful rider could be very competitive on those bikes against factory sponsored riders. But it always helped to have the very latest factory innovations.

Mike knew he would be asked to test ride. That meant he'd be working with engineers and other riders on new products. His dream for a life time career was to go to college after his racing career ended. He wanted to become an engineer with a motorcycle company. In his mind it all depended on the results of the next moto.

He listened as the 125 cc. class went off the line for their second race. It was a sound that was pleasant to his ear. He felt no matter how old he was or how many years away from racing he was he would always be thrilled at that sound.

He must have drifted off for a short nap as Bill gently tugged at his jacket. "Up and at 'em, Tiger. You must be really relaxed if you can sleep between motos."

Mike smiled up at Bill. "I wasn't asleep, I was just resting my eyes."

"Yeah, right," Bill teased. "If I didn't wake you up, you'd be snoring by now."

"What a cool cucumber your son is, Ann, he's over here sleeping before the biggest race of his life.!" Bill said with a laugh.

"How much time have I got, Bill?"

"Enough, if you start getting dressed right now. And don't forget your stretching exercises."

"Gotcha, Buddy."

Mike began pulling his gear back on. He felt strong and rested. His extra time spent lifting weights, wrestling and running as well as the laps around his practice track was paying off now.

Motocross Mike

His recovery time was amazing. He felt he had never been in such great shape.

He finished dressing and moved around the bike. Bill had gone over it with a fine tooth comb, totally cleaning it and checking every nut and bolt. The engine was tuned and adjusted.

It was time to move towards the start gate and Bill pushed the bike to the start area. Other riders moved aside to let Mike move towards the front of the pack. He had come in third and would be the third rider to pick his spot on the line. One by one the riders were called. Again, Mike picked a spot towards the middle and they moved the bike into place.

The start area was considerably more chewed up than it had been for the first moto. Mike liked that because he could make out the consistency of the dirt better and see any hidden rocks. Bill grooved the dirt in front of Mike's bike to give him good traction.

Mike straddled the bike and kicked it over. It barked to life ready to go as the other riders started their bikes too. He twisted the throttle on and off to warm the engine and looked up and down the line at the other riders. Seemingly relaxed, they all assumed a dignified, alert appearance. Mike knew better. He knew that the apprehension and excitement flowing through his veins was the same for everyone..

Charles Loomis

Careers were on the line. Money and status were on everyone's mind. The older riders were hoping for one more season, maybe two. The younger riders yearned to move up into the slots held by the aging veterans.

Bill patted Mike on the back. "Be tough, kid," he said as he moved to go to the mechanics area.

Mike nodded and gave Bill a "thumbs up".

Mike was confident but he was feeling the pressure. This was the "big one". How he performed here would make the difference in how he was thought of by the decision makers at Honda. He had a lot at stake.

Mike watched as the starter raised the board and held up the "2" sign. His heart began to pound. The board was turned around and the big number "1" was displayed. Bikes jockeyed into the final positions, the riders stood on tip toes, leaning forward and cranking the throttles off and on to a higher and higher pitch. The "G" forces would be strong on the riders arms when the clutches were released and the extreme forward position was necessary to prevent the bikes from looping over backwards when fresh rear tires "hooked up".

Mike was ready when the starter dropped the gate a split second after the board went sideways.

He popped the clutch out and was off. His start was perfect. He hit the first turn before any of the other riders. As he rounded

Motocross Mike

the first turn he could see a pack of riders go down right behind him, but he was free. He had no idea who or how many went down, but he did know that it gave him some precious time to ride a clear track and open up a lead. Any rider wanting to challenge him would have to use up precious energy to close that gap.

Mike rode faster than he had ever ridden before. No riders pressuring him meant that he had his pick of the best lines on the track. He never backed off one bit. He knew that Sanders, Buel, Collins and other experienced riders would be right on his tail in no time at all. He could hear his fans yelling and screaming as he passed near them on different sections of the track.

He rocketed past a jumping and screaming Bill in the mechanics area. The fences and spectators flew by in a blur. He was flying off the jumps in spectacular cross ups and in complete control. He was really enjoying himself.

Near the start area he looked around as he rounded the sharp turn there. He could make out three riders moving in behind him. He knew this would happen. The more experienced pros moved within striking distance. He still had a big enough lead to make it to the finish line. He kept pushing as hard as he could.

The four man freight train continued around the course, Mike in the lead and Collins, Sanders and Buel following close behind jockeying for the next three spots.

Charles Loomis

And then, almost before he could believe it, it was over. Mike finished in first place with Collins, Sanders and Buel close behind.

He had won his first professional race.

Mike took the checkered flag and stood up on the pegs punching both fists in the air. He took off his goggles and flung them into the rampaging crowd. His fans had stampeded to the finish line area to see Mike win. The crowd trampled a fence and poured through the opening towards Mike.

They were totally out of control but Mike didn't care. He was as excited as they were. It wasn't often that they saw a hometown rider win at Unadilla.

He sat back down on the seat and rode off in a long, slow wheelie through a back gate in the pit fence. He found Bill's van and hoisted the bike up on the stand as he ran to embrace his mother. He lifted her off the ground in a big bear hug and swung her around.

"We did it, Mom, we did it!" He said over and over. Bill came running up and joined their happy dance. The fans had crowded up to the fence near the van and were chanting. "We like Mike! We like Mike!" It was a wild and happy scene.

Moments later, Mike strode to the podium with his mother and Bill. He climbed to the middle stand, the highest one. The

Motocross Mike

second and third place finishers, Sanders and Buel, stood on either side of him.

Champagne corks popped and flew through the air into the crowd. Everyone was soaked in champagne.

Mike grabbed the microphone and thanked Bill and his mother and paid compliments to Buel and Sanders for a close, clean race.

The three posed for pictures and then stepped down. Buel and Sanders each took turns giving Mike a pat on the back and wished him well. Sanders rode for Honda and he moved close to speak quietly in Mike's ear. "Don't tell anyone I told you, but I think I'm going to be seeing a lot more of you. Congratulations."

Mike looked up and saw Hugh Black and Jim Hawkins, the two Honda factory reps moving towards him. They were smiling and Hugh was waving a paper and pen so Mike could see it.

A new world was opening up. Mike was about to become a factory sponsored racer. The race had ended, but his dream was just beginning.

-----END-----

About The Author

In his career as an elementary school principal in Amsterdam, New York, Charles Loomis was always on the lookout for high interest level books for young readers. Discovering that they were in short supply, he decided to write his own middle grade action books.

Drawing on his twenty some years of amateur dirt bike racing in Enduros, Hare Scrambles and Ice Racing, and cruising the trails in his beloved Adirondack foothills he is crafting a series of action/adventure books for young readers.

He also has a keen interest in other motor sports and is working on action/adventure books based on Auto Racing.

Charles lives in New York in the Adirondack Mountains and takes great pleasure in sailing on the Sacandaga Lake. We are sure that an adventure book on sailing will be forthcoming.

###

Printed in the United States
43596LVS00001B/73